THE OC

SPRING BREAK

SCHOLASTIC INC.
New York   Toronto   London   Auckland   Sydney
Mexico City   New Delhi   Hong Kong   Buenos Aires

MW01027996

No part of this work may be reproduced in whole or in part, stored in a retrieval system, or transmitted in any form or by any means, electronic, mechanical, photocopying, recording, or otherwise, without written permission of the publisher. For more information regarding permission, write to Scholastic Inc., Attention: Permissions Department, 557 Broadway, New York, NY 10012.

ISBN 0-439-69632-1

12 11 10 9 8 7 6 5 4 3 2   5 6 7 8 9 10/0

Designed by Louise Bova
Printed in the U.S.A.
First printing, March 2005

1

Breathe, Ryan reminded himself, staring out the window, trying to quell the panic rising in his throat. *Everything's fine, nothing bad's going to happen, just keep breathing.* Outside the window, the grass was still green, the sky was still blue, only — there was more sky than usual, and the grass was getting farther away every second. . . .

Ryan tore his eyes away from the rapidly disappearing ground and looked around the plane.

How could all these people be so calm? Didn't they realize that they were hurtling through the air in a huge metal box? Physics be damned! It just didn't make sense that an 800,000-pound plane could stay up in the air.

He glanced out the window again — Jesus, where had the ground gone? They were actually in the middle of a cloud! How could the pilot see where they were going? Even if the plane didn't just drop out of the sky like the incredibly heavy thing that it was, if the pilot couldn't see what was in front of him, they could run into a mountain or get lost and circle until they ran out of fuel or — could they run out of oxygen? Ryan realized he had no idea how they were able to breathe so high up in the atmosphere where there was no air — actually, Ryan suddenly realized he wasn't breathing, so he gasped hugely, trying to suck in as much oxygen as possible before they ran out.

Seth, who was happily reading a comic and listening to a Kill Hannah CD on his iPod, glanced over at Ryan, noticing how weird his friend was acting.

"You okay there, buddy?" he asked, slipping off his headphones.

Ryan nodded, not trusting himself to speak. Seth shrugged and got up to go to the bathroom. Ryan used the moment of privacy to rummage through the seat pocket in front of his, searching for the card printed with the safety instructions.

He studied the location of the emergency exits: three rows in front of him. He'd climb right over the seats to get to it if he had to. Not exactly chivalrous, but extreme circumstances called for extreme measures.

Ryan checked for the millionth time that his seat belt was fastened, then wiped the sweat off his forehead. He hadn't told Seth that he was afraid of flying. This was only his second time on a plane. The first had been when he flew to Portland to see Seth. Then he'd been too worried about how he was going to persuade Seth to come home to think about what he was doing. This time, as excited as he had been when Sandy offered to take them to New York City for spring break, he was beginning to wish he'd just stayed home.

Spring break. Two words that conjured up visions of girls in bikinis, wet T-shirt contests, drunken hookups on the beach, sunburns and margaritas and fun, fun, fun in the minds of boys all across America. Ever since they got back to school after Christmas vacation, the kids at Harbor had talked of nothing else. Where would they go? What hotel would they stay at? Who would they go with? And for the majority of the class, Cabo San Lucas was the only acceptable answer. Cabo had the best beaches, the hottest girls, the most lax ID policies. Everyone who was anyone was headed down to Cabo for eight perfect days. Everyone, that is, except . . .

"Screw Cabo," Seth had said when Ryan had brought up the fact that if they wanted to stay in a good hotel, they should probably reserve a room early. "Cabo sucks. Why would I want to spend my week off staying in a hotel with all the same jerks we see at school every day, being rejected by all the same girls who reject me here? We need to go somewhere cool."

He had a point, Ryan realized. If the entire school was going down there, there was a really good chance that Marissa was going to be there, too. And while they were doing all right being just friends, it didn't mean he wanted to see her

3

making out on the beach with some other guy. That would not help their burgeoning friendship one bit.

But where else could they go? "We could go to Miami and stay with the Nana," Seth suggested.

"Yeah, and maybe we'll get lucky with some of the foxy senior babes in her retirement village while we're there," Ryan answered dryly.

"Okay," Seth responded. "What about going to visit Anna in Pittsburgh?"

"As much fun as spending a week watching you mack on Anna would be, I'm gonna have to say no," Ryan said.

Seth blew his breath out, exasperated. "Well, do you have any better ideas?"

"I have one," Sandy said. He'd walked into the kitchen to get a beer, and as he flipped the cap off it, he smiled at the boys. "I'm going to New York for some meetings — if you boys want to come along, we could make a week of it."

"Really?" Seth said, his eyes lighting up. "Oh my god. Oh my god! Finally, I'll return to the land of my people."

"Your people?" Sandy asked, amused.

"Have you seen a Woody Allen movie?" Seth asked his dad. "All those Jewish neuroses? I'll be like a god there."

Sandy laughed and turned to Ryan. "Sound good?" he asked.

Ryan grinned. "Sounds perfect."

* * *

If only he had stopped to think that New York was thousands of miles away, he wouldn't have agreed so readily.

Seth came back down the aisle from the bathroom, squeezing past the pretty blond flight attendant who was wheeling the drink cart down the aisle. Sandy was up in first class — courtesy of an upgrade from Kirsten's AMEX card — but the boys were stuck in coach. *The "death seats,"* Ryan thought miserably.

Seth paused in front of their row and stared down at the safety card that Ryan was still clutching. "What are you —" he started, then his eyes took in how pale Ryan was, the way his fingers were gripping the card as though it were the one thing keeping him from plummeting back down to the ground. A grin twitched around the corners of Seth's mouth as he realized how Ryan was feeling.

"Dude, when I was coming out of the bathroom, I saw the pilot tipping back one of those little bottles of vodka. I think he's drunk."

Ryan sighed, realizing he'd been made. "You did not —" he said, but all at once the plane lurched, as if confirming Seth's words. The seat-belt light blinked on, and the plane jostled again, sending a couple of the cans of soda on the flight attendant's cart rolling haphazardly down the aisle.

Seth slipped into his seat and fastened his seat-belt as the captain's voice came booming over the loudspeakers. "We're experiencing a bit of turbulence," he said in a calm, deep voice. "Please return to your seats, and things should clear up soon."

Seth relaxed, but Ryan stiffened, his fingernails digging into the fabric of the armrest the boys shared. With each jounce, Ryan let out a little yelp.

"I never should have gotten on this plane," Ryan whispered, abandoning all attempts to stay cool in front of Seth. "We're all gonna die."

"Not necessarily," Seth said comfortingly, patting Ryan on the arm. "Maybe it'll be like that movie *Alive*, where that rugby team crashed in the Andes and had to eat one another. Whaddaya think, Ry? If we go down in the Rockies, would you resort to cannibalism to stay alive?"

"We're not going to crash in the Rockies," Ryan said, trying to convince himself as much as Seth. He shut his eyes and concentrated on not throwing up.

"I don't know — there really is an awful lot of turbulence." Seth bounced up and down in his seat, making the entire row rock. "All those movies and TV shows about plane crashes? Always start with turbulence."

"Seth —" Ryan said in a warning voice, but Seth ignored him.

"*Lost, Castaway, Airport 77, The Crash of Flight 32,* uh . . . *George of the Jungle* . . ."

Ryan opened one skeptical eye. "You're honestly trying to scare me with *George of the Jungle*?"

"Okay," Seth said, thinking hard. "*The English Patient*. That's a bad one. I'd rather be a cannibal than be terribly burned when we crash." Seth glanced at Ryan's green face and laughed. "Seriously, dude, you gotta prepare yourself. We might have to bail out."

"Shut up!" Ryan lunged at Seth, fully planning on throttling him, but the second Ryan let go of the armrests, the plane lurched, hitting another pocket of turbulence. Ryan felt his stomach drop away and let out an agonized little shriek. He clutched the armrest again with one hand, his other involuntarily reaching for Seth's hand.

Seth looked down at the white-knuckled fingers grasping his wrist and smiled. Maybe he should take pity on the poor guy, give him a break. Then again — how often did he have the upper hand?

"At least I'll be the last one eaten," Seth said, proudly flexing a scrawny bicep. "That's why I keep myself sinewy. Just in case."

Ryan shut his eyes again, trembling. If they made it out alive he was going to kill Seth Cohen.

2

Marissa was also sitting on a plane trembling, but that's where the similarity between her and Ryan ended. For one thing, she was relaxing in the first-class cabin on a plane headed toward Maui, and she wasn't trembling from fright but from excitement.

She hadn't seen Jimmy since Christmas, so when he invited her to visit him over break, she jumped at the chance. She glanced over at Summer, who was sprawled in the seat next to her, sipping champagne and giggling over the fashions in the stack of glossy magazines they had picked up at the John Wayne Airport in the O.C. before getting on the plane.

Thank god Summer was coming with her. As excited as she was to see her father, part of Marissa was nervous. She held up her champagne glass so the flight attendant could refill it and thought back to the last conversation she'd had with Jimmy.

"Did you get the guidebook I sent you?" Jimmy had asked. "You should pick out some things you want to do and see while you're here, so we can plan ahead."

"Okay," Marissa had told him, "but it doesn't matter what we do. As long as I get to spend time with you I'll be happy."

"Me too, sweetheart," he'd answered. "I'm taking off work, so we'll have the entire week together. You're going to love it here. And Morgan's spent weeks fixing up your room just right."

Morgan was Jimmy's new girlfriend. He'd mentioned her a bunch when they talked, but this was the first time Marissa realized that Jimmy and Morgan were serious enough that she was helping him decorate. She wasn't — she wasn't living with Jimmy, was she? No, Marissa decided, if Jimmy were going to move in with someone, he'd definitely tell her first. Jimmy probably just let Morgan fix up her room because he was notoriously aesthetically challenged. He'd only been living in Hawaii for a few months — Marissa figured she'd be lucky if he'd managed to buy a couch and table, let alone decorate the place.

"Morgan's dying to meet you," Jimmy continued. "We can't wait until you get here."

"Me too," Marissa said vaguely, hanging up the phone.

She didn't mind her father dating, especially now that he and Julie were officially, definitively over. But just because she didn't mind, it didn't mean that she wanted to hear about it. Parents should keep their private lives private. Nothing was worse than imagining your mom or dad getting it on with a date. Ugh. Marissa shuddered just thinking about it. And in Jimmy's resolve to stay involved with and close to his daughter, he tended to talk about things that Marissa would just as soon not hear.

Nothing outwardly gross, of course. Marissa couldn't imagine a world where Jimmy would mention sex in front of her, but at the same time, even hearing about his feelings and emotions was a little scary, and god forbid that he'd want to discuss how she was feeling about him dating again.

What she needed, Marissa decided, was a buffer. Someone to take the pressure off, to help her avoid overtly sentimental or candid moments with her father. Someone . . . like Summer.

Summer had come along on half the vacations the Coopers took, anyway, so it'd be completely natural and unsuspicious to bring her. But as much as Jimmy adored Summer and thought of her almost as a second daughter, Marissa knew that he'd be far more likely to steer clear of the deep stuff with her in the room.

Besides, Summer was great to travel with. She was always up for anything, and it was a lot more fun having someone to go shopping with and tell you when you're starting to burn and stay up all night giggling when you should be asleep.

Marissa finished her second glass of champagne, then reached over and gave Summer an impulsive hug. "I'm so happy you're coming with me."

"Are you kidding?" Summer answered. "There is nowhere I'd rather be."

Marissa actually had almost not asked Summer to come, because she assumed Summer would want to spend the break with Zach.

"Everybody assumed that, including Zach," Summer said, looking disgruntled. "But I thought maybe we should take spring break literally — take a break from seeing each other every day and talking on the phone every night."

Marissa's eyes widened. "Do you want to break up with him?"

"No," Summer answered, twisting a lock of her hair in nervous knots. "I mean, I don't think so. It's just . . . more and more lately, things about Zach that I used to think were cool or funny or endearing just seem . . . annoying."

"Like what?"

"Oh, you know. Stupid things. Like, he opens his eyes really wide whenever he has something to say."

Marissa laughed. "You're going to break up with him over *that*?"

"Not just that," Summer protested. "He also programmed the ring tone on his cell phone to play 'Summer Lovin'' from *Grease*."

"That's kind of sweet," Marissa said, and Summer shrugged.

"Maybe at first. But now anytime anybody calls him, he sings the whole stupid song and gets all pissy if I don't do the 'tell me more, tell me more's'.

It just gets on my nerves. Plus, he has this stupid little sneeze like a kitten, which completely skeeves me out. And his hands are always rough and chapped, which wouldn't bother me that much, except he acts like he's a character from a Hemingway story whose hands got torn up fighting bulls or wrestling grizzlies or something."

"I think that's kind of hot," Marissa said. "Rough hands — it's rugged and . . . masculine."

"If he'd gotten them from working! But Zach? His hands are just dried out because he's on Accutane."

"No way," Marissa said, giggling. "He's got acne?"

"All over his *back*," Summer said, starting to laugh, too. "But you can't tell anyone — he's totally embarrassed about it."

"I'll keep it secret," Marissa promised. "But seriously, Summer, is all that really reason enough to want to break up with him?"

"I don't know," Summer said quietly. "I'm not sure what I want anymore."

Cohen's hands were rough, too, Summer thought, but that was from sailing. He earned those hands. He deserved them. Lately, Summer had been thinking about Seth Cohen more and more often. Maybe too often. And that was one of the reasons she had so readily agreed to go to Hawaii with Marissa. She wanted a week away from the boys in her life, so she could try to figure some of this stuff out. Because it was impossible to try to sort out how she felt about Zach when she had to see him all the time.

But she couldn't get it all to make sense while she was still on the plane. "I need to figure it out, but not right now. Just thinking about it makes me itchy."

"Well, then let's think about something else," Marissa said matter-of-factly. She pulled out a copy of *In Style* from their stack of magazines and flipped it open to a fashion spread featuring Jude Law. "Let's think about him."

"That I can do," Summer said, and the two girls bent their heads over the magazine as the plane carried them away from the O.C. and all their troubles there.

3

While Ryan and Sandy waited at baggage claim for their suitcases to finally come tumbling down the chute, Seth dashed into the newsstand at the JFK terminal and bought a copy of *Time Out New York*, the weekly magazine that gave the scoop on everything cool happening in the city.

The three guys piled into the back of a yellow cab, and Seth opened the bag he'd bought. He pulled out the magazine and a bunch of candy bars. He passed one to Sandy, but Ryan declined — as rough as the plane ride had been, it was nothing compared to the nightmare of landing, and Ryan wasn't sure his stomach was up for chocolate just yet.

Seth shrugged and, pulling off the foil, stuffed half the bar into his mouth at once as he flipped through the magazine to the music section. "Oh my god, look at this," he said, amazed. He held the magazine up so Ryan and Sandy could see page after page of listings — clubs showcasing every sort of music you could imagine. Rock, punk, pop, blues — "Metal rockabilly?" Seth read. "We have got to go see this band."

"You don't like metal or rockabilly," Ryan said. "Why would you want to see a combination of both?"

"Because it's at CBGB's," Seth said. "Only the home to some of the greatest bands in the history of music."

"I thought that was the Vienna Opera House," Sandy commented. Ryan grinned, but Seth wasn't listening.

"My god, some of these clubs have bands around the clock. There's nothing like that in Newport Beach. Or even Los Angeles."

"It's the city that never sleeps," Ryan said, looking out the window as the cab sped down the freeway. So far everything just looked sort of gray and industrial. Maybe the crowds and the skyscrapers were only in Manhattan. What he really wanted to see was the Statue of Liberty, but he was embarrassed to admit he wasn't sure exactly where to look for it. He hoped that maybe they'd drive past it on their way to the hotel.

"Listen to this: On Tuesday at Arlene's Grocery, there's an all-day concert featuring the Malcontents, Hot Carl, and the Rusty Trombones."

"They're playing at a grocery store?" Ryan asked, and Seth frowned.

"That's what it says — maybe that's the name of

the club or something. Anyway, it'll be totally cool. That's what we're doing on Tuesday, okay?"

"Sure," Ryan said.

But Sandy shook his head. "Or . . ." he said, and the two boys looked at him expectantly.

"Or what? What could possibly be better than paying tribute to some of the greatest musicians of our generation?"

"You could get to know them firsthand," Sandy said.

The boys glanced at each other, unsure what he was talking about. Sandy smiled mysteriously and didn't say anything else. He looked out the window and hummed, building the anticipation. Seth was the first to crack.

"Dad! What are you talking about?"

"I called up Robert Bollinger, one of my old college buddies, to let him know I was coming to town, and it turns out he's an executive at MTV. He said he's got a couple weeklong internships at the studio that he's looking to fill, so if you two are interested, you can spend the week getting a behind-the-scenes look at how the network is run."

"No way!" Seth tugged at the collar of his green-striped polo shirt, stretching the neck out of shape as he beamed at his father. "That would be the coolest thing ever!"

"Yeah," Ryan agreed. "Besides, it'll give me something to put on my college applications besides bussing tables at the Crab Shack and spending time in juvie."

Seth grinned and held out a fist for Ryan to bump. "Look out, New York, the O.C. is in the house."

4

The Hawaii Tourist Board spared no expense. The Maui airport was full of welcoming hula dancers, and Marissa and Summer were both heaped with leis before Jimmy even reached them. "Aloha!" he belted out, grabbing Marissa for a big hug.

"Dad, it's so good to see you." Marissa sank into the hug with relief. How silly she had been to worry that the distance between her and her dad would hurt their closeness. Of course, it would only help them appreciate their time together more.

Summer got an equally enthusiastic squeeze. "Hey, Mr. Cooper. Thanks for moving to the best place on the planet," she told him as Jimmy hoisted Summer's sizable carry-on. Summer beamed, thoroughly at home with the Coopers. "'Cause much as I love you both, spring break in Buffalo would have been out of the question."

Jimmy laughed. "I'm happy to say that rumors of paradise have not been exaggerated. You are both going to have a fantastic time."

In the car, Summer's head practically hung out

18

the window. "Hawaiian palm trees are so much cooler than the ones back home," she gushed.

Marissa sat in the front, clutching Jimmy's arm excitedly.

"So, you girls have anything special on your agenda?" Jimmy asked. "Because there's a thousand and one things to do here and I won't presume that you're going to share my idea of a good time."

Marissa made a face. "No, Dad. Seven days on the golf course is not how we intend to spend spring break."

Summer piped up from the backseat, "We really ought to learn how to play, Coop. When we get older, all the hot, rich guys are going to be hanging out on the golf course."

Marissa made a snoring sound.

Jimmy responded, "You know, my interests actually have expanded since I've been here. That's right — you turn your back long enough and your old man might even turn into an interesting guy."

Marissa gave him an affectionate nudge. *Parents worry too much about being hip and cool to their kids*, Marissa thought. *He can turn into a shuffleboard fanatic for all I care. Still, if he's up for a little adventure . . .* "If you really want to expand those horizons, how about we go parasailing?" she suggested.

"Where they take you up in the air?" Jimmy asked.

Marissa nodded, and Jimmy turned pale.

"But they make you go up really high. I mean, *really* high."

Summer laughed.

Marissa flipped through the pile of brochures she had nabbed at the airport. "Then might I suggest a little scuba diving?"

Jimmy flinched.

"Oh, come on," Marissa begged. "It's supposed to be amazing here. Clear water, amazing fish."

Jimmy shook his head. "You know, a woman was killed in a shark attack on the beach here."

Both girls gasped.

"Oh my god, when?"

Jimmy was hoping they wouldn't ask. "Oh, it was about . . . seven years ago."

The girls erupted in peals of laughter, which Jimmy pointedly ignored.

"You know what, Mr. Cooper," Summer said, clutching her sides, "I think that shark is probably dead."

They arrived at Jimmy's house in high spirits. It was a modest size, nothing like their old family house in Newport Beach. But it had a real island feel to it. All the room that a bachelor needs, with a little extra space for visiting loved ones. Marissa nodded approvingly. *This is going to be my second home — who knows, maybe for the next ten years. Dad will probably still have this place after I've left for college, and I'll still be coming here to visit him.*

These thoughts filled Marissa with warm comfort. The past year had been so full of turmoil and separation and insecurity, it was great to see Jimmy settling into a secure place. It made her life feel that much more secure as well.

The front door burst open, and a thin, pretty, blond, forty-something woman stepped out. "Oh, don't tell me. She's got Jimmy written all over her," she said, pulling Marissa into a hug.

Marissa tensed up, but plastered on a smile when the woman pulled away.

The woman turned to Summer, pumping her hand warmly. "And you must be Summer."

Jimmy grinned. "Girls, this is Morgan."

Both girls smiled and said hi, Summer more enthusiastically than Marissa.

Morgan held the door open for them. "Come on in. I think you're gonna like your rooms. We've been working so hard to get things ready for you two."

Marissa didn't like the sound of this. *Why should she work so hard for us? She doesn't even know us. And she and Dad have only been going out for, like, two months. I hope she's not planning on tagging along on all our trips.*

The inside of the house was pure Martha Stewart. The fresh cut flowers were color coordinated with the carpeting. The paintings, the curtains, the armoire . . . Either Jimmy had just handed $20,000 over to a great interior designer, or Morgan had been there 24/7 transforming his bachelor's pad into a cozy domestic retreat.

Marissa realized how irrational her discomfort was, and yet, she couldn't help it. She had expected to find her dad in the midst of a transitional period of his life, and here he was, a whole new life already in full swing. And Morgan was obviously a big part of it.

Summer was oblivious to Marissa's uneasiness. "Mr. Cooper, I'm impressed. Marissa had me expecting two notches above dormitory hell."

Jimmy put his arm around Morgan. "You have Morgan to thank for the gorgeous accommodations. She's turned this place into a real home."

Marissa drew in a sharp breath. "It's great," she said weakly.

Then came the big tour: the guest rooms, the office, the art deco bathroom, the Mediterranean villa bathroom. Summer's oohing and aaahing was loud enough that Marissa hoped her own lack of enthusiasm went unnoticed. They arrived at the master bedroom, and Marissa stopped short.

What if the room was filled with Morgan's clothes and belongings? Jimmy hadn't said anything about Morgan living there, but the awful thought had crossed her mind several times since their arrival. Did she really want concrete evidence of just how serious her dad and Morgan were? Marissa took a deep breath before stepping through the door her father held open for her.

The room had a comfortingly masculine feel. But she had to be sure. "Are these walk-in closets?" she asked innocently.

Swinging the closet door open, she was immediately relieved to find an all-male wardrobe inside. *At least Morgan had somewhere else to go home to*, Marissa thought. Maybe all she needed to do was to drop a few hints about being tired and Morgan would give her and Jimmy a little privacy for their first day together.

Morgan came up behind Marissa. "That's the one drawback of this place. They didn't plan for a lot of closet space. Or much storage space downstairs, either. We've had to add so many wall units to compensate."

Marissa felt her chest tightening. *WE?!! What's up with the we?!! My father and I are we. GO HOME!!*

Of course, Morgan wouldn't take the hint. She had prepared sandwiches and lemonade for the girls and was happy to preside over the afternoon lunch. "We have to take the girls to Haleakala," she told Jimmy, then turned to Marissa. "It's a national park that you will just flip over. It's this beautiful little oasis in the hills, and it's got these waterfalls. Oh, you will just love it."

Marissa recognized the name of the place from her tourist brochures. It was definitely on the list of places she wanted to see, but just her, Dad, and Summer. *I am not going to spend my entire vacation with this woman!*

Summer gave Marissa a sharp poke under the table, jolting her upright. Marissa realized she had been staring off into space, lost in thought for a good five minutes while the conversation was going on around her, and Morgan and Jimmy were both staring at her strangely.

"So, Morgan, what do you do?" Marissa said politely, hoping the thoughts she'd been having weren't apparent on her face. Maybe Morgan had some kind of time-consuming job that would keep her out of the way.

"I'm a hotel manager at the Marriott. I make sure that everything's beautiful and running smoothly. And I'm such a people person. It's perfect for my personality."

Jimmy smiled at Morgan, resting his hand on top of hers. "Did I luck out or what? She has put my whole life in order like you wouldn't believe. I don't know what I did without her."

Marissa tried to shrug this off and get back to her only hopes for salvaging the week. "You probably have to get to work pretty early in the morning?" she asked.

But Morgan flashed a big smile. "I took the week off, too, just as soon as your dad told me you were coming. I couldn't miss out on the big family vacation. I have so many things planned. We'll sit down after dinner and work out a nice itinerary."

Itinerary? Do I look like a hotel guest?

Summer, oddly enough, was thrilled to have a tour leader. Morgan's promise of filling every waking hour with activity was the perfect antidote to boys on the brain. Besides, Summer loved good luxury accommodations, and this had to be the next best thing to actually staying at the Marriott.

Marissa had to get away from everyone, or she was going to have a meltdown. "I'm going to go for a walk. I really need to stretch my legs after that plane ride."

"Oh, I'll come with you —" Morgan started, but Marissa cut her off.

"That's okay, you should finish your lunch. I won't go far."

"Go ahead, sweetheart. It's a beautiful neighborhood," Jimmy responded. Marissa could tell that no one had detected her turbulent state of mind. But she didn't know whether that made her irritated or glad.

THE

5

They checked into the SoHo Grand Hotel, Ryan and Seth sharing a suite with two queen-sized beds across the hall from Sandy's room.

"Nice and firm," said Seth, sitting on the edge of his bed and bouncing. "Just the way the ladies like it."

"What ladies?" Ryan asked, testing out his own bed.

"All the hot, lonely New York girls who have just been waiting for some Cohenization."

"Cohenization?" Ryan said, shaking his head. "I don't really think —" He broke off as Seth held up a warning hand.

"Don't say it," Seth warned. "We are in a city of eight million people. That's four million women, most of them Jewish, who don't know anything about me except I'm single, handsome"— Ryan snorted, but Seth ignored him —"and ready for action."

"And exactly where are you planning on finding these desperate girls?"

"Are you kidding? They're all over the place —"

"— Waiting for you."

"Yep," Seth said, checking out his reflection in the mirror over the desk. He turned to face Ryan and flashed his most winning smile. "It's like Fleet Week's come early, and this sailor's ready to make all their dreams come true."

Ryan laughed, then clapped his friend on the back. "Then let's go get 'em."

They met up with Sandy in the lobby, where he was shouting into his cell phone. When he saw the boys, Sandy held up a finger, signaling them to wait while he finished his conversation.

He finally hung up his phone with an annoyed snap. "Change of plans," he told them. "I need to go into the office here for a couple hours — I'm sorry, I'd wanted to take you guys sightseeing."

"That's okay," Seth said. "Will you be done in time for dinner? 'Cause maybe me and Ryan could just hang out in the Village and meet up with you tonight."

"Sounds good," Sandy said. "And maybe we can hit the Empire State Building tomorrow morning, before you boys start your internships."

"The Empire State Building?" Seth said derisively. "That's for tourists."

"We are tourists," Sandy answered. "Anyway, the view from the top is unbelievable. You can see all of Manhattan."

"Besides," Ryan reminded him, "you know what happened in the Empire State Building?"

"What?"

"Kavalier and Clay published *The Escape Artist*," Ryan said, referring to Seth's favorite book. *The Amazing Adventures of Kavalier and Clay* was the story of two cousins who start a comic book empire out of an office in the Empire State Building. Ryan couldn't believe that Seth had forgotten the reference. He only talked about the book constantly, and practically the only thing Seth and Ryan fought about was the fact that Ryan had never managed to read the entire 636-page tome.

"My god, you're right," Seth said in awe. "We're in the city of Kavalier and Clay. We should make a pilgrimage to all the places listed in the book. The Trevi, the Perisphere —"

"— Antarctica," Ryan chimed in.

"I don't think the Perisphere exists anymore," Sandy said, "and I'm not sure we'll have enough time to hit all those other places."

"We could just check out St. Mark's Comics and call it even," Ryan suggested, and Seth sucked in his breath.

"Mecca," he whispered. And agreeing to meet Sandy back at the hotel in three hours, the boys tumbled into a cab and set out to explore the city.

They spent an hour in St. Mark's Comics, Seth spending all the money he had in his wallet on comic books. They walked around the East Village for a while, poking their heads into the little shops and stands that lined the streets, then headed over to Astor Place.

"Think I should get a haircut?" Ryan joked as they looked in the window of the Astor barbers, which was crowded with street kids getting their heads shaved into Mohawks and dyed colors not found in nature.

"Better than getting that —" Seth responded, tilting his chin at a boy coming out of a pizza place, covered with so many tattoos it looked like he was wearing a turtleneck.

The kid noticed Seth's gesture and smiled. "Boo-yah!" he said, and disappeared down into the subway. Ryan and Seth looked at each other and burst out laughing.

"These are 'your people,'" Ryan reminded Seth, and gave him a friendly elbow to the ribs.

The two boys crossed Broadway and walked down Waverly Place to Washington Square. There were tons of people in the park enjoying the warm spring sunshine: college girls lounging on benches, getting a jump start on their tans, cool slacker guys playing with pooches at the dog run, little kids chasing squirrels across the paved walks to the amusement and exasperation of their mothers.

Ryan and Seth passed through the great stone arch at the north side of the park and made their way to the pit where a crowd of people was gathered, hollering and cheering at the action in the ring. They pushed their way through the crowd to discover two skate punks jousting.

One boy had shaggy blue hair and was wearing a ripped Thrash Monkeys T-shirt; the other had a scraggly beard and a small silver hoop piercing his eyebrow. The punks both wore BMX padding for armor and were on opposite sides of the circle, glaring at each other as they strapped on their helmets. They raised their lances — a broom and a mop, then mounted their skateboards.

"No way," breathed Seth as a freaky goth girl walked to the center of the ring. She held a surprisingly clean white handkerchief over her head and dropped it.

At once, the skate punks were off. Their feet pushed off the concrete as they aimed their boards at each other, lances held taut before them.

Ryan and Seth stood riveted, their eyes glued to the scene in front of them. In seconds, the skate punks made contact. *Bam!* The blue-haired kid's mop smacked his rival in the center of his chest, and the pierced kid went down.

"Ouch," said Ryan, wincing in sympathy.

The crowd erupted in cheers as the winner skated around the arena in triumph. Seth and Ryan clapped loudly with the other spectators, but Seth leaned over to whisper a criticism of the fallen skater's performance in Ryan's ear. "He held his center of gravity too high. If he'd bent his knees, he could've stayed on his board."

The goth girl, who had retreated to the edge of the crowd to stay out of the jousters' way, smiled up at Seth. "Want to go next?"

"What?" Seth asked, looking slightly panicked.

"You seem like you know what you're doing," she said, plucking at his sleeve with one blue-fingernailed hand, in a gesture that could be either flirty or bossy, depending on how you looked at it. "Anyone can joust. We do this all day."

"I don't have my board," Seth told the girl, apologetic but relieved.

But she shouted across the pit to a grubby teen boy with a shaved head. "Yo, Rat. Lend this kid your deck."

"Hang on —" Seth started, but the girl ignored him.

Rat strolled over to them, a battered skateboard and jousting gear loosely tucked under his arm. "This kid know how to skate?" he asked the goth girl.

"Hell, yeah," she said. "He's the best skater in the five boroughs."

"Then let him prove it," Rat said, and he shoved his skateboard into Seth's arms.

Seth shot a look at Ryan, who shrugged. "Uh, I don't know the rules," he said to the goth girl.

"It's easy," she said. "Two rules: number one, knock that other guy down. Number two, don't get knocked down yourself."

"I don't know," Seth said, looking like he wished they'd gone to Cabo after all.

"You have padding," the goth girl said, "so you won't get hurt. Besides, you're going up against Jason — he's a total wimp."

"He's a crier," Rat said, and let out a short bark-ing laugh.

The goth girl looked at Ryan to back her up. He took the broom-lance from her and ran a hand over its bristles. "You do know all about that center of gravity stuff," he said, and Seth grinned, suddenly decided.

"Let me at 'em," he said. The goth girl squealed and clapped, and Ryan helped Seth on with his padding and helmet.

When Seth was all suited up, he grabbed the broom and climbed onto the borrowed skateboard. He skated into position and faced his challenger. Jason might have been a crier, but he was a *big* crier. Like, two hundred pounds big. Seth wiped his sweating palms on his jeans leg and gripped the broomstick tighter. He glanced over at Ryan, who gave him an encouraging thumbs-up.

The goth girl walked to the center of the ring and checked to make sure Seth was ready. He gave her a nod, and she lifted the handkerchief high again. Blowing him a quick kiss, she let it drop.

Instantly, Seth was off. He shot across the ring with an ollie kick-flip, landing easily to the impressed murmurs of the crowd.

Jason, who had been expecting the standard front-on collision, looked around in confusion.

Seth came up behind Jason and, using his broom as a lever, slid up the edge of the pit in a perfect caballerial. He landed squarely in front of Jason and, before the big guy had a chance to react, tapped him in the chest with the bristles of his broomstick.

Caught off guard, Jason went down, and the crowd went crazy.

The goth girl ran up to Seth and wrapped her arms around him, and Ryan and Rat were slapping him on the back, thrilled by his victory.

"Man, that was something," Ryan said.

"Piece of cake," Seth said, but his flushed cheeks and broad grin gave away how excited he was. "Now we better hurry, or we're going to be late meeting Dad for dinner."

Seth finally managed to extricate himself from the swarm of well-wishers, and he and Ryan made their way out of the park. They'd reached the edge of the park when a shout made them turn back.

The goth girl came running up and pressed something in Seth's hand. "A souvenir," she said and, blushing, raced away.

Seth looked down at his hand — it was the white handkerchief used to start the joust. He gave a little smile and tucked it in his pocket.

Ryan stared at him in amazement. "That girl," Ryan said, "has been Cohenized."

"First of many, my friend," Seth said, and the two boys headed out of the park.

6

The greenery at the local park went a long way toward calming Marissa. Flowers were in full bloom everywhere and the air was thick with their fragrance. *Free aromatherapy,* she thought. The cute guys playing Frisbee were also a welcome distraction. Shirtless and very athletic. Marissa was always relieved to be reminded that she could be attracted to other boys beside Ryan. Speaking of, he was probably in New York right that minute scoping out girls to hook up with. Definitely not the kind of guy who would be spending spring break without a wide selection of willing female companionship. Well, Marissa certainly wasn't going to be the moping loser here. Time to have a little romantic adventure of her own.

The level of Frisbee expertise in the park was pretty high, so when a Frisbee "accidentally" landed two feet away from the bench Marissa had settled on, she took it as a friendly compliment.

A boy with dark brown hair, deep dimples, and

a swimmer's body approached. "That didn't hit you, did it? 'Cause if it did, I will kick Billy's ass."

He and Marissa both laughed. "I'm Kyle, by the way," he added.

"Marissa."

"Marissa. You're not from around here."

"How can you tell? Do Hawaiian girls look so different?" Marissa asked flirtatiously.

Kyle looked her up and down with a straight face. "It's the shoes." He plunked himself down on the bench next to her.

"These are Jimmy Choos," Marissa started defensively, but Kyle's grin stopped her.

"Exactly. Hawaiian girls only own shoes that they don't mind wearing into the ocean," he said.

"Then I'll have to go shopping and buy some," Marissa told him. "I don't want to stand out."

"You would stand out no matter what you had on," Kyle answered, his dark eyes twinkling.

From across the park, Kyle's friend Billy waved and headed for his car. "Very unsociable guy," Kyle explained. "Me, on the other hand, I like to give newcomers a big aloha."

Oh my god, Marissa thought. Kyle was sweet, he was adorable, and he had such an easygoing way about him — miles away from Ryan's moodiness.

"Are you visiting someone on the island?" Kyle asked.

"Yeah. Me and my friend Summer came to see

my father. He just moved here about six months ago," Marissa answered.

Kyle looked so understanding that before Marissa knew what she was doing, it all came spilling out.

"But it looks like it's going to be a pretty terrible week, actually," she blurted. "My father just started seeing this woman. I mean, that's always a little strange. Are your parents together?"

"Divorced. A long time now," Kyle responded.

"So, of course, you have to get used to the whole dating thing," Marissa continued, "but she's one of these women who just completely takes over everyone's life. She does it with a smile on her face and this nauseatingly innocent domestic-diva vibe. But, I swear, she has this whole plan mapped out."

Kyle chuckled. "World domination?"

"That's not too far from the truth. My father's a pretty successful business guy, and I know she sees him as this big meal ticket. Her key to the good life. So, he's going through this 'poor me, lonely bachelor' thing, and she swoops in with her homemade scones and flower arrangements. Before you know it, my father has talked himself into being in love, she's got the ring on her finger that she's been drooling over, and as soon as the ceremony is over, all the pretense is going to drop away, and I am going to turn into the one blemish in her otherwise faultlessly designed plan." Marissa paused and sucked in a long breath, surprised at her own vehemence.

Kyle shook his head in mock sympathy. "Cinderella, Cinderella."

Marissa joined his laughter, but she was not really joking. "If you met her, you would know I was not exaggerating."

"Sounds like you could use a little diversion. Could I talk you into a horseback ride? Tomorrow afternoon?" He gave her a quick glance, then teased, "At least it'll get you out of the house and away from the future stepmonster for a few hours."

Marissa lit up. "I haven't ridden a horse in such a long time. That would be perfect."

"Cool," Kyle said. "Why don't I walk you home now, so I know where to pick you up tomorrow?"

"'Kay," Marissa said, and they started down the street.

They chatted casually for most of the walk, but when they turned onto Jimmy's street, Kyle got a strange look on his face. By the time they turned into Jimmy's driveway, he was completely silent.

"Do you mind coming in? My dad won't let me go out with a guy I just met in a new city without a little screening."

"Um —" Kyle stammered, but Marissa turned her most winning smile on him and grabbed his hand.

"Come on — he won't bite," she said, and pulled him into the house.

Jimmy and Morgan were snuggled up on the couch, reading the paper together. Marissa swallowed her annoyance at the sight and opened her mouth for the introduction. But Kyle was the first to speak.

"Hey, Jimmy. Hey, Mom."

Mom? Marissa froze, shock and anger rising up inside her. Morgan, the woman she'd been complaining about for the last hour, was Kyle's *mother?* Unbelievable.

Morgan and Jimmy looked pleasantly surprised to see the two of them together. "Kyle honey, how did you two run into each other?" Morgan asked.

"At the park, actually. Although it wasn't until we walked up the drive that I was able to confirm that this was the same Marissa I've heard so much about." Kyle smiled at Marissa's growing dismay.

Morgan leaped up. "Well, now that you're here anyway, which sounds better for dinner — lasagna or paella?"

Kyle glanced mischievously at Marissa. "Mmmm. Lasagna. Now that's the ticket"— he paused for a beat, then added, in a significant-sounding voice — "the *meal* ticket."

Marissa glared back at him, mortified. How on earth did she wind up on this vacation from hell?

7

Sandy's work took him out of the hotel early the next morning, so after a quick breakfast in the hotel's restaurant where they decided to try to hit the Empire State Building another day, Sandy left the boys to find their own way to the MTV building in midtown.

Ryan and Seth went back up to the suite to try to figure out what to wear for their first day of work.

"Uh, jeans and a T-shirt," Ryan decided, grimacing at his suitcase. That was all he'd brought! But Seth had six different shirts laid out on the bed and was trying to decide.

"I want to look hip, but not like I'm trying to look hip," he said.

"Oh, then the stripes, definitely."

"Really?" Seth said, gazing doubtfully at the shirt in question.

"Absolutely," Ryan responded. "It's very *GQ*. Very *Queer Eye*."

"Yeah?" Seth picked it up and, giving it a cursory shake to ostensibly knock out any impending wrinkles, slipped it on and started buttoning it up.

"Yeah," Ryan confirmed. "Very *Teen People*."

Seth glanced over at him and saw the smirk threatening the corners of Ryan's mouth. "Jerk," he said, throwing a rolled-up pair of socks at Ryan's head and missing by a mile. "This is important."

"Yeah, but come on. 'Hip but not trying to look hip'? What are you, a girl?"

"Shut up!" Seth said.

"Sorry," Ryan said, not looking sorry at all.

"I wonder if they have valet service here," Seth mused, reaching for the phone to dial the concierge. "Maybe I could get this pressed, holding up one of the shirts from the bed."

"We don't have time," Ryan said, and Seth nodded.

He looked at himself critically in the mirror. "Today could be the start of my life as a rock mogul, and I'm going to look all creased."

"Look at it this way," Ryan said, clapping his friend on the shoulder. "How many alt rockers do you think worry about their outfits?"

"Some," Seth answered petulantly.

"You think Kurt Cobain cared if his shirt looked sloppy?"

"No," Seth conceded, "but look how he turned out."

Ryan and Seth stood on the sidewalk in front of the hotel, waiting for an empty cab to come by to pick them up, but every one that passed was full of passengers. Finally the doorman noticed the boys and came down to talk to them.

"Can I help you gentlemen summon a cab?" he asked, also peering at the traffic down the street.

"Yeah, thanks," Ryan said. "We need to be at MTV at ten."

"Their midtown offices?" the doorman said, with a concerned glance at his watch. "You'll never make it in this traffic."

"I told you we were late," Ryan said with a furious glance at Seth, who shrugged sheepishly.

"What should we do?" Seth asked, and the doorman smiled reassuringly.

"Subway'll take you right to the corner," he said, and pointed the boys to the nearest stop.

They walked to the subway entrance, and Seth stopped.

"What?" Ryan asked, already halfway down the steps.

"Maybe we should just wait for a cab," Seth said, looking around to see if one would miraculously pull up at that exact second.

"There's no time," Ryan said, starting down the steps again.

"Wait," Seth said. Ryan looked at him, and when Seth didn't say anything else, gestured impatiently.

"We're going to be late."

"I know, but —"

"Seth, what?!"

"Subways are dangerous. I don't think we should take it."

Ryan looked at him — he was serious. "What do you mean, they're dangerous?"

"People get killed on the subway all the time!"

"What, like from being pushed onto the tracks in front of a train?" Ryan asked, and Seth blanched.

"Oh my god, I hadn't even thought of that," he said. "I was thinking more of the roving gangs who terrorize the trains."

Ryan looked around at the people entering and exiting the subway stop. An elderly lady in pearls, a couple of preteen girls in plaid Catholic school uniforms, a well-groomed man in a Prada suit.

"Roving gangs?" he repeated, and Seth nodded. "There are no roving gangs."

"Yes, there are," Seth insisted. "May I remind you of a little movie called *Death Wish*?"

To Seth's indignation, Ryan burst out laughing. "Come on, Charles Bronson," he said, and headed down into the subway.

Seth hesitated, then raced after his friend. "Ryan! Wait up! What about *The Warriors*? There were roving gangs in that movie, too. In lots of movies!"

Five minutes later, they were seated on the train, surrounded by middle-aged women.

"See?" Ryan said. "Nothing to worry about." The words were no sooner out of his mouth when the door between cars opened and an immense, thuggish-looking man shoved his way into their car. He sat down on the bench directly across from Seth and reached into the rumpled paper bag he was carrying.

Seth and Ryan both stiffened — what was in the bag? A gun? A knife? A tense moment passed, then the man pulled out — a library copy of *The Da Vinci Code*.

The thuggy man opened the book up and started to read, and Seth and Ryan relaxed.

Ryan leaned over and in Seth's ear singsonged, "Warriors, come out and play."

Seth didn't stop laughing until they reached their stop.

They got to the MTV building without incident and waited in the lobby, bursting with excitement, for Sandy's friend Robert to come meet them.

Moments later, they were in the elevators, ascending to the internship office on the twenty-second floor, where they were met by a cool-looking kid dressed all in black whom Robert introduced as Marco.

"Marco is my right-hand man," Robert explained. "He coordinates all the interns and can answer any questions you might have. Why don't you let him give you the tour, then meet me back here and I'll give you your placements."

Ryan and Seth nodded, and Robert strode away down the hall. Marco waited until he had disappeared from sight, then turned to the boys.

"Hey, guys," he said in a casual drawl that sounded more like a surfer from the O.C. than a

Manhattan hipster. "First thing you need to know is that if you think you're going to be working one-on-one with the bands, forget it. Those sorts of assignments are rare, and they're almost always given to the boss's niece or someone like that."

"Really?" Seth said, struggling to hide his disappointment.

"Well, usually, so unless you got some kind of pull with the big guy, you better prepare yourself for intern hell, otherwise known as the mailroom."

"What would we do in the mailroom?" Ryan asked, and Marco laughed.

"Deliver mail. Receive mail. Mail out mail. Really, anything in the mail universe. Put stamps on things. Sign for packages. You get it."

"I get it," said Ryan, and he made a face at Seth as Marco led them down the hall to begin their tour.

The MTV offices were really cool. While a lot of the work space looked like ordinary cubicles, the walls were all painted with rock murals, and a lot of the common spaces had Ping-Pong and Foozball tables in them. Marco stopped in a small kitchen area and handed each of the boys a Coke, then continued toward the elevators.

"We'll go check out the studios now," he told them. "Just be careful not to make any noise if there's a red light flashing. That means they're recording."

The three guys walked through a gigantic door onto a darkened soundstage. There were lights and camera equipment piled against the walls, and

Seth and Ryan recognized the set from the MTV news segments. They passed onto a different stage, made up to look like a living room, and as they entered a third, the red lights began to flash.

Marco put a finger to his lips and led them silently into the room. The set was decorated to look like a beach, with colorful umbrellas and a volleyball net, and sitting in the middle of a blanket spread out on the sand was Milla MacNeil, lead singer of the Cutters, one of Seth's favorite bands!

Seth's mouth dropped open in delight, and only a warning look from Marco reminded him not to make any noise.

Milla was facing the cameras, introducing her five favorite videos. "I'll count one down every day this week," she said in her trademark Scottish accent that made Seth go weak in the knees. "I'll be your guest VJ all this week, so stay tuned to MTV!"

The cameraman signaled to her, and Milla relaxed, getting to her feet and taking a long drink from a bottle of Evian. The red lights stopped flashing, and Marco smiled at the two starstruck interns.

"Yeah, the Cutters are going to be here until Friday." He paused, then grinned mischievously. "Want to meet Milla?"

"Are you serious?" Seth asked, and he and Ryan exchanged excited looks.

"Sure," Marco drawled. "Come on."

He walked up to Milla, the two boys trailing behind him, and held out his hand for her to shake.

"Hi, Milla. I'm Marco, and these are a couple of our interns, Ryan and Seth."

Milla looked up at the boys from under her long dark lashes. Her green eyes sparkled as she shook each boy's hand in turn.

"It's an honor to meet you," Seth said, then instantly felt foolish. But Milla paused, taking him in, his hand still warm in hers.

"Nice shirt," she said and, as she turned away to talk to the cameraman, winked at him.

Seth literally staggered backward, clutching at his chest as though his heart were going to burst right out of it. Milla MacNeil had winked at him! She liked his shirt! Oh my god — Seth couldn't believe how much he liked New York. NYU instantly rose to the top of his college wish list. If he had it his way, he'd never go back to the O.C. but stay in the Big Apple forever.

He sat down on a pile of crates and looked around the studio, smiling. He could get used to this. In a second.

Ryan walked over to him, looking grouchy. "I knew I should have worn something other than a T-shirt," he scowled.

Seth was still laughing when Sandy's friend Robert came down to the set and spotted them. He wandered over to them and cocked an eyebrow.

"Learning your way around okay?"

"Absolutely," Ryan answered. "This is great — everyone, the studios, it's all really fantastic."

"Glad to hear it," Robert said, and straightened his tie, grinning at the two boys. "Now, Marco might have told you that we usually assign interns to the mailroom."

"Yes, sir," Ryan said, and Seth nodded.

"Important job," Robert continued. "Nuts and bolts of this place. I started in the mailroom myself. However —"

Ryan and Seth shot a glance at each other. *However?*

"— Milla MacNeil needs an assistant for the week, someone to make sure she's got everything she needs, take care of her, keep her happy."

Seth felt the blood drain out of his face. This was beyond his wildest dreams. Spending a week hanging out with one of his favorite bands? It was beyond good.

"So why don't you plan on that," Robert said, pointing at Ryan. "— And you" — Seth —"can go with Marco down to the mailroom to get started."

Seth blinked. Ryan? Ryan was going to hang out with the Cutters, while Seth was stuck toiling away in mailroom obscurity? He blinked about twenty times in a row, trying to wrap his head around the fact that his perfect dream had just been stolen from him.

Ryan was smiling and shaking hands with Robert, who told the two boys to grab some lunch before they reported to work, but Seth was frozen, still unable to process the huge, unfair catastrophe that was his life.

"He seems cool," Ryan said as Robert walked away. "You want to head down to the cafeteria and grab a bite?"

"No," Seth said, and Ryan looked at him.

"You aren't hungry?"

"No," Seth repeated, then shook his head to clear it, blinking a bunch more times. "No, I mean, *no*, there is no way in the world that you are going to spend the week hanging out with Milla instead of me."

Ryan kept a complete poker face as he looked at his best friend. The second Robert picked him, he knew Seth would want to swap jobs. And to be perfectly honest, he didn't really mind switching — Seth was way more into the whole music thing than Ryan was. And Ryan wasn't sure that playing run-and-fetch for some girl was the ideal way to spend his vacation . . . even if that girl was a beautiful rock star.

So Ryan knew he would trade jobs with Seth, but he hadn't forgotten how Seth had tormented him on the plane ride to New York. Now seemed like the perfect time for a little payback.

"I don't know, man," he said, slowly shaking his head and staring at the floor, a perplexed expression on his face. "Robert assigned me to the band. He might get mad if we switched."

"He won't get mad," Seth said. He felt like screaming at Ryan to change jobs with him, like taking him by the shoulders and shaking him until he agreed to switch, like locking him in a closet for the rest of the week so he couldn't do the assistant job.

48

Ryan shrugged. "Even if he doesn't get mad —" He paused for a long beat, watching Seth out of the corner of his eye. Seth was turning bright red and practically vibrating with jealousy. "I just think I'd probably be better at being an assistant to the band than you."

"Are you kidding?" Seth shouted. "I've been working at The Bait Shop for months."

"Sure, cleaning toilets and mopping up spills," Ryan said. "You don't actually talk to the bands, though."

Seth took a deep breath, struggling to keep himself under control.

"What," he asked through clenched teeth, "is it going to take for you to swap jobs with me?"

Ryan stared off into space, considering. When he finally decided that if he waited any longer, a blood vessel in Seth's brain would probably pop and kill him, Ryan relented.

"Nothing," he said with a shrug. "We can switch jobs if you want to."

He headed down the hall toward lunch, Seth's whoops of delight carrying him all the way to the cafeteria.

8

Marissa walked down the stairs cautiously. The coast was clear. No Morgan in sight. Marissa hadn't been sure if she was going to have to endure a sleepover, but her father's common sense had obviously prevailed. If Morgan had spent the night in the house, it would already smell of freshly ground coffee and pancakes from scratch.

Speaking of which . . . Marissa would love to start cooking something, but Jimmy was not in his room, and he wasn't in the house. Maybe he went to pick up some bagels. Best to wait till he got back.

Unfortunately, the wait gave her more time to stew about yesterday's events. Dinner was insufferable. Morgan was just fluttering around the table, unable to settle down until her food had been sufficiently praised. Giving Jimmy a little back rub every time she passed him. Marissa got the very unsettling idea that Jimmy was so happy in his new life that he probably didn't have time to even think about his own daughter, much less miss her.

Here she had been worried that Dad was cut off from everyone he loved, and the familiarlarity of his old life. Trying to start life again at his age! Frozen dinners. Thanksgivings volunteering down at the soup kitchen to comfort himself by helping the less fortunate. Of course, Marissa hadn't wanted her father to be miserable. But she always assumed that she was an important part of his happiness, and now she was feeling totally expendable.

Summer entered. "How ya feeling, grump?"

Marissa's grimace confirmed that her frame of mind had not improved. Summer plopped down near Marissa. "You're away from Ryan. You're away from your mother. You've been dying to see your dad, and here he is, in a great mood. He'd do anything for you that doesn't involve extreme sports. And hello . . . we're in Hawaii. So what's the deal?"

Marissa knew how completely feeble her problems would sound, so: "There's no deal." She shrugged, in an attempt at nonchalance.

But Summer wasn't fooled. "Take two Midol and call me when breakfast is ready. I'm jumping in the shower," she called as she headed for the stairs.

Marissa was relieved to be alone again. If being with Summer didn't cheer her up, then what chance would she stand with Dad? Or Morgan? Or Kyle? Kyle! He must have known or at least suspected that she was talking about his mother when they met at the park.

During dinner, he continued what he must have

thought was a good-natured ribbing of Marissa, but it felt to her like being stretched on the rack. It was the longest sixty minutes of her life. It also turned into Sports Central, with Jimmy and Kyle going over the basketball season, play by play.

Morgan joined in enthusiastically, of course.

Marissa understood that she was simply feigning this huge interest in sports to help convince Jimmy that she was the perfect woman. *She plays him like a puppet. Why am I the only one who sees it? And what if they do get married??!!! Morgan! Kyle! I can't even think about it. I wonder if . . . I wonder if . . .*

What Marissa wondered was whether or not there was any alcohol in the house.

She had already polished off the little bottle from the plane. There had been a bottle of red wine at dinner, but Marissa had passed it up, mindful of Jimmy's watchful eye. She had told her parents that she wasn't drinking at all. Just so that they wouldn't worry. Besides, the small amounts that she drank now were no big deal.

Even now, it just seemed impossible to make it through the day without getting stressed out. The sight of Ryan. Fights with her mother, and knowing that she had tried to put Marissa in an institution once and might very well try again. Nightmares of Oliver holding a gun to her head. The whole overdosing thing . . . and coming way too close to death.

There were times when alcohol seemed like a

miracle cure. A pill for forgetfulness. Now, a couple of drinks seemed like one of the few things that could make this vacation week fly by.

Marissa was startled by the arrival of her father and Kyle. *No, not at eight-thirty in the morning. That's just wrong.* But what was even more wrong — "What are you wearing?" Marissa said, staring at Jimmy's unusual attire.

"I told you the old man had a few new tricks up his sleeve. We've been out riding." Jimmy was delighted by Marissa's confusion.

"Out riding. Riding in the Jeep? Riding . . . No! Not riding horses?!!"

Jimmy bragged, "I have to say, I think I'm a natural. I mean, we've gone out now, what — about ten times?" he asked Kyle.

"At least a dozen times. You're cowboy material now. We need to head to Makawao next weekend. They've got this old-style Wild West outpost. You'll get such a kick out of it."

Marissa was still dumbfounded. "You were never interested in riding before. I asked you over and over again, and you wouldn't even give it a try."

Jimmy seemed surprised that Marissa even remembered that. "That was ages ago."

"It was four years ago. I was thirteen."

This sent Jimmy off into his own little reverie. "Four years ago. Man. That big house, and that pressure at work, and that whole social circle we had to keep up with. God. My life is so much better now in every way."

Jimmy had no idea how these words fell on Marissa's ears. She had been part of that old life . . . the one he apparently hated so much. And the world he was waxing rhapsodic about now? That one barely included her.

Jimmy's attention floated back to Kyle. "Your mother's a great sport. But I can't really see her on a horse."

Kyle agreed. "She's not that fond of four-legged creatures, no. But horses are especially *not* her thing. I got her on one once, though. Wait'll you see the picture. She looks as terrified as if she were sitting on an alligator."

Jimmy laughed and patted Kyle on the back. "Now I have you to do that stuff with. Shoot hoops. Go fishing."

Marissa turned away. *Fishing?* She had always felt so secure at being Daddy's little girl that she never noticed that apparently what Daddy really wanted was a little boy.

Why was it that when she had once begged him to share her love of riding, he couldn't be bothered? But now he wanted to be John Wayne? And hoops? I could play hoops. No, it's not my big thing. But if he had asked, of course I would have played with him. Dad has only known Kyle for less than eight weeks and he already . . . likes him better than me.

It was a devastating but undeniable realization.

Jimmy was having a blast with Kyle. Morgan took up every remaining moment of his free time, and life in California was a distant — and inferior — memory for him. Marissa fought hard against the lump in her throat. She was not going to make a scene.

Kyle sidled up to her. "You are joining us for the luau at Mom's hotel tonight, aren't you?"

Marissa recoiled. "Roast pig with an apple in its mouth? Very appetizing, but I think I'm gonna pass."

Jimmy looked surprised. "But Summer is really looking forward to this, honey."

"Summer is free to do as she pleases. And so am I," Marissa said, determined not to budge.

Kyle and Jimmy exchanged a look, finally aware that all was not well.

Kyle tried again. "I know we were going to go riding today —"

"But you must be all tuckered out," Marissa interrupted. "Don't worry on my account. I'd really rather spend a quiet day here."

Kyle countered, "No, I had an alternative in mind. I got an e-mail last night, and a group of my friends are headed out sailing today. It would be great if you and Summer could join us."

Marissa folded her arms stubbornly. "Like I said, Summer can do as she pleases. I'm really not in the mood for sailing."

Jimmy saw that it was time for him to step in. He gestured apologetically. "Kyle, have a seat. I'll get some coffee going for us. Marissa, could you give me a hand in the kitchen?" It was clear from his tone of voice that this was more command than request. Marissa followed him defiantly.

"Is there some sort of problem here?" Jimmy demanded.

Marissa whirled around to face him. "Yeah, how about me flying out here to spend some time with you? Not Kyle. Not Morgan. You! But I don't know if you're going to be able to squeeze me into your schedule."

"My schedule! What schedule?" Jimmy was genuinely clueless.

"Well, are you going to that luau tonight?"

"Uh, I was planning on it, yeah." Whatever was bugging Marissa, Jimmy knew he just made it worse. "Okay, kiddo, I'd like to propose Plan B. We send Summer off to pig-fest, and you and I go score a lobster at one of these fine local establishments."

After a split second, Marissa couldn't keep back a smile, her first since setting foot in this house.

But Jimmy wasn't finished. "As a gesture of goodwill, however, I am going to insist that you spend the afternoon in the grueling, arduous, and unpleasant occupation of sailing the sparkling blue seas in the company of an attractive young group of your peers."

Marissa's smile disappeared. This quid pro quo sucked. But at least she would have her dad all to herself tonight. She gave in. "Deal."

9

Ryan and Seth stood at the edge of the cafeteria holding their plastic lunch trays, looking for a place to sit. The cafeteria was crowded with groups of people who all seemed to have known one another forever, and who didn't seem particularly interested in welcoming newcomers.

"My god, it's worse than Harbor," Seth said, searching for a couple of free chairs. "At least at school I can eat lunch in the library if I'm not in the mood to be ignored."

"Maybe we should —" Ryan started, but was interrupted by someone calling his name.

"Ryan! Seth! Over here!"

They looked over to a table in the far corner of the cafeteria, where Marco was sitting with a group of kids all dressed in jeans and T-shirts. They made their way over and sat down, smiling gratefully at Marco.

"Tucker, Brad, Diane, Carson, Emily," Marco said, pointing at each person in turn, "this is Ryan and Seth, our newest interns."

"Hey," Seth said, and Ryan sketched a wave as the other interns said hello.

"How do you like it so far?" one of the girls — Diane? Ryan couldn't remember — asked, taking a sip of diet Coke and smiling at them.

"It's amazing," Seth said.

"It's . . . big," Ryan added.

"You'll get used to it," Diane said reassuringly. "When I started, I used to get lost every single time I left the mailroom. It'd take me an hour just to drop off a package to someone, or to find the ladies' room, but after only a couple days, I was walking around like I owned the place."

"How long have you been working here?" Ryan asked.

"Since the beginning of the semester. Do you guys go to NYU?"

Seth shook his head. "We're just in for a week from California."

"L.A.?" one of the boys asked through a mouthful of tuna fish.

"Orange County," Seth answered.

The boy put down his sandwich. "No way. I spent a month surfing in Oceanside last summer. You ever make it to Beacon's Beach? The waves are so sweet there — oh no. You guys, here comes Leah."

All the kids at the table groaned. Seth glanced around to see Leah, a cute but goofy-looking girl who walked up to the table. Her hair was pulled tight into two sloppy braids, she was wearing a

"Reduce, Reuse, Recycle" T-shirt, and was carrying a small potted tree.

"Hi, gang!" Leah said, flashing her smile around the table.

"Hi, Leah," Marco answered. He was the only one who did.

"I just wanted to remind you all to be sure to put your empty pop cans in the green barrels after lunch. If we recycle fifteen hundred cans, we'll raise enough money to plant five trees outside the front entry," Leah said.

She held up the potted tree to demonstrate. The interns sitting around the table snickered.

"Why should we care about the entryway?" Brad asked. "All of our internships end in May."

Leah rolled her eyes. "We all breathe the oxygen, Brad."

Emily opened her eyes really wide, staring up at Leah in horror. "Wait a minute — you're collecting cans? Like a homeless person?"

"It's called recycling. Maybe you've heard of it?" Leah set the tree on the table for a second and Emily reached out a cautious hand to touch the leaves of the tree. All the interns sitting at the table giggled.

"Oh my god, Leah, is this a marijuana plant?"

But the derision was so plain on Leah's face that Seth had to smile. "It's a Korean boxwood," Leah said patiently.

"It looks like marijuana. You're going to be in big trouble if anyone sees you."

"It's not marijuana. It's a Korean boxwood."

"Leah Goldman growing marijuana," Brad said, shaking his head sadly. "What is the world coming to?"

"It's not —" Leah started again, but then gave up. "Look, just put your pop cans in the green barrels, okay?"

Diane stood up. She swallowed the last sips of her diet Coke and handed the empty can to Leah. "Will you recycle mine for me?"

"Sure," Leah said, taking the can.

Diane turned to the rest of the interns at the table. "Come on, guys. They're showing the newest *Real World* episode in the screening room — let's check it out before we have to get back to work."

The other kids stood up, piling their soda cans into Leah's arms and walking away. Diane turned back to Ryan and Seth. "Coming, guys?"

Ryan smiled apologetically at Leah, then grabbed what was left of his lunch, sliding it into the bus tray before following his new friends out the door.

Leah took a step toward the recycling bin, but the movement was too much for the mountain of cans in her arms. With a crash they dropped to the floor. Leah bent down to pick them up, and Seth knelt down next to her to help.

"Thanks," Leah said, dropping the cans in the bin and wiping her hands off on a paper napkin.

"Those guys are jerks," Seth told her, and she smiled at him.

"Yeah," she agreed. "But the kids at my school are just as bad, so I guess I'm used to it."

"Do you go to NYU?" Seth asked, and Leah shook her head.

"I'm still in high school. I go to Worthington, on the Upper East Side."

"I'm in high school, too," Seth told her. "In California."

"You came all the way out here to work at MTV?" Leah asked, and Seth nodded.

"Are you kidding? I'd go halfway around the world to get to work with the Cutters."

Leah shrugged, and Seth raised an eyebrow at her. "Come on. You must love music as much as I do to put up with those assholes on your spring break."

"I do," she admitted. "I just wish I got to see more of the bands themselves."

"Are you stuck in the mailroom?"

"I'm in the *accounting office*," she said, in a voice that implied it was a fate worse than death.

"Wow," Seth agreed. "That sounds really boring."

"Usually it is," Leah said, and a sudden smile lit up her face. "But some days it's not so bad."

Seth smiled back, his hands full of discarded soda cans. *Already this trip has been so worth it*, Seth thought. *I can't imagine anything that could spoil this for me.*

10

The *Blue Rose* was a huge sailboat. It could sleep four, and on this particular afternoon, it was carrying a crowd of eight teenagers: one girl besides Marissa and Summer, and four guys besides Kyle. Marissa was not happy to see the sex ratio. The fewer girls there were, the more she would be expected to socialize and that was the last thing she wanted. SPF 30, a good paperback, and as much solitude as could be found on a fifty-five-foot piece of plastic slicing through the Pacific — that was all she needed to make it through the next four tedious hours.

How could she have forgotten to bring her earphones? The inane conversation that drifted her way was going to drive her nuts. "So, he got together all these crazy-looking bugs, just like in those reality shows, and said that he would give his old car away to whoever was the first to swallow two of the bugs. Oh my god. You should have seen it." The other girl, Ellie, had this high-pitched squeal, and the thought of guys puking in the attempt to swallow live insects was evidently her idea of premium humor. Marissa didn't know how Summer could put up with them.

Summer's mind was actually hundreds of miles away. The last time she had been around a sailboat had been with Cohen. They were still a couple then and they had been in the middle of one of their particularly stupid-happy periods. She had hung out on the dock while he worked, and they talked *and* talked. About what, Summer could hardly remember. In retrospect, that was the crazy thing about Seth. As completely different and totally incompatible as the two of them were, they never ran out of things to talk about.

Oh, sometimes he annoyed her with those esoteric topics that he was constantly thinking about. *At least I know what esoteric means now. Dating Cohen was like preparing for the SATs. Ubiquitous, obsequious, insidious, dichotomy. How could I possibly have dated a boy who had vocabulary going for him? Vocabulary!!* Not the kind of boy you could have fun with.

Well, not true. Summer's mind strained to block out all memories to the contrary. Especially memories of his hands and lips, which were remarkably talented, out of all proportion to the rest of his skinny frame.

Summer forcefully dragged her attention back to the boisterous group in front of her. These boys were spectacularly cute. And this was the perfect opportunity to find out if Zach really was the best guy out there for her, or if she could find a lot of other guys equally appealing.

Kyle approached Marissa waving a white handkerchief. "Olive branch, anyone?" Marissa knew that this would have been the perfect opportunity to put the past behind them, be a good sport, play nice, blah, blah, blah. But the whole father-son dynamic of the morning was still grating on her.

"I suppose you told your mom what I said about her."

Kyle sat down right across from Marissa. "What? That insufferable gold-digger! You know, now that I think about it, she probably got pregnant to trap my father into marrying her, just to get ahold of that primo schoolteacher's salary of his."

Kyle had the upper hand with Marissa, but she didn't want to let him know that she cared. "Go ahead. Tell her. She'll run to Dad. He'll get pissed off at me and hustle me right back home."

Kyle tried to calm Marissa with a touch on her arm, but she pulled away.

"First of all, I would never tell her. I mean, she's pretty easygoing, but the whole scheming, conniving wicked stepmother thing, that she might have a little bit of trouble with. And second, your dad is not going to send you packing for any reason. He's a great guy. He's an amazing guy." Kyle had hoped to win a few brownie points with some mutual positive feelings about Jimmy, but he couldn't have been more wrong.

"Do you think I need you to tell me that my

64

father is a great guy?" Marissa shouted over the wind. "There's nothing you can tell me about my father. You don't know anything about what this past year has been like or everything he's been through. But I guess that's some kind of bonus. You're just a completely fresh start. You've never given him a moment's worry and you don't remind him of anything bad that has ever happened to him. My ex-boyfriend slept with his ex-wife. Maybe that's one of the things that he remembers whenever he sees me. And that's the least of it. That is just the tip of the Cooper iceberg."

Kyle's jaw had dropped. "Whoa! Just hold it right there. Just, just . . ." He shook his head, knowing that nothing coming from him could possibly make Marissa feel better. "You know, I get it. I can't do anything about it. But I get it. My parents split up when I was eleven. And it stinks, and it hurts, and you hate them, and the whole dating thing just seems too cruel and unusual. I totally get it." He stood up and stepped away.

Marissa curled up against the rail as far away from the others as she could get. *No, you don't get it.*

Summer marched up to Marissa in disbelief. "What exactly is it about the concept of fun that you don't understand?"

Marissa pulled Summer down to the deck. "You're right. I don't understand what part of this outing is supposed to be fun. But, why don't you sit with me for a while? Maybe that will keep anyone else from coming over."

Summer pointed over at the boys, who were all looking in their direction. "What you and I are going to do is to go back over there and give those guys a day that they'll still be drooling over when they're paunchy and middle-aged. . . .

"We're hot, Coop. It's a burden. And it comes with certain obligations.

"If Ted Kaczynski had been hot, he could never have been the Unabomber. So get a grip, stop mooning over Ryan, and join the party." Summer returned to the crowd, with a backward warning glance at Marissa, who turned away.

Swell. I hadn't even been thinking about Ryan.

Teddy, Ethan, and Lewis. As far as Summer was concerned, this was the finest-looking assortment of boys she had come across in a long time. There was one kind of gangly, awkward guy steering the boat, Ben, but the rest were smokin'. Including Kyle, who now had Ellie hanging all over him. Was Marissa crazy? This could have been the best spring break ever if she would only come to her senses.

"Hey, Summer, you've got to come to this party tonight. It is so going to blow your mind." This invitation came from Lewis, the bug-eating enthusiast.

He was also a football player, but according to him, he was getting a bum deal as far as college recruitment, because the scouts were only prepared to go to states where they could look at several prospects.

"See, that's totally working against me, because, really, I am the only pro-level high-schooler in this state."

"Bummer, dude," Teddy offered.

Summer, however, was getting tired of the whining. Zach didn't whine. Oh, just about the usual stuff. Parents, and homework, and too much reading to do, and how his science teacher wouldn't let him retake the midterm, and, whatever . . . Maybe he did whine a little. Everyone did.

What did Seth whine about? Summer did her best to remember. He was certainly unpopular enough to have a lot of complaints with the world. But he talked about being so lucky. Summer flinched at the thought. *He thought he was the luckiest guy in school because of me.* Which one of these guys, Summer wondered dubiously, would think that dating her would be an end to all his dissatisfaction with life?

Ethan was in a band and wanted to fill everyone in on his latest high-voltage acquisitions. Teddy was an expert on cars. Summer loved riding in really cool cars, but hearing them discussed ad nauseum only sent her mind wandering again. Funny how you could put the nods and giggles on autopilot, and no one suspected that you'd checked out of the conversation.

Even though a few things about Zach were currently getting on Summer's nerves, these guys were sort of irritating her from day one. Good guys to go to movies with, and be seen with at dances — *not* an unimportant consideration. But they actually made her think a little wistfully of Zach. Which was great. That was exactly what Summer needed to be clear about.

Ethan was rattling on about his band. "So, we're trying out all these bass guitarists, and one of them is just killing, and . . . oh, hey, it looks like Ben wants to get off the wheel." Ethan took over the steering from Ben, who took his place. Kind of a toad next to the others, but maybe he'd at least have something interesting to say. That was one of Summer's new theories. Homely guys try harder to be interesting. What else have they got?

Kyle managed to extricate himself from Ellie and was taking another stab at connecting with Marissa.

"So, got any plans for the summer yet?" he inquired.

"I'm not planning on coming back here, if that's what you're asking," Marissa snapped.

"Not at all. I just meant, what are you doing? Job? Traveling? Great American novel? Just wondering."

Marissa regarded him suspiciously. "Did you promise your mother, or my dad, that you would make sure I had a great time? Because I'm perfectly prepared to lie through my teeth and say I had the world's best time. So, you're off the hook. You can go back to your girlfriend now."

Kyle glanced back at Ellie, who was now draped around Lewis. "Not my girlfriend. And I know all those guys really well. It's you I don't know. What's your school like? What's your mother like? What do you do for fun?"

From Kyle's perspective, these were pretty harmless questions, but he should have known better.

"Why are you trying to get to know me? I'm only going to be in your life for a week and then I'm out of here."

"That's not really true. You're always going to be Jimmy's daughter."

It only took a minute for the implication to hit Marissa. "*What?* And you think that he's a permanent part of your life now? And you need to get to know me because you think we're going to be some kind of family?!!"

Marissa was so incensed by the thought that she leaped to her feet and stormed away.

Not quite what Kyle had in mind, but at least he got her to move.

All of Kyle's friends had moved to Hawaii with their families in the past five years. They all still tripped over some of the Hawaiian names. Which reminded Summer of something she'd read about in the guidebook last night, while waiting for Marissa to get home from her walk, and hiding out from Jimmy and Morgan, who were doing more on that couch than Marissa ever needed to know about.

"So, did you know that Hawaiian gods were all real actual people? Summer turned and asked the group. "Not like the Greeks or Romans, who made up their gods to explain science and uncertainties, but in Hawaii, the people who were respected and revered in their lifetimes were actually deified after their deaths. So, yeah, the Hawaiian gods were all once real normal people."

No, none of them was aware of this historical bit of information and really didn't know what to make of it. They gaped at Summer as if she were conducting a chemistry lab.

Damn that Cohen. He would find this interesting. He's ruined me for other guys by molding me with his geek influences. It was part of a master plan. An insidious master plan.

Marissa finally made her way across the boat, winding up near Ethan at the wheel. She couldn't help but notice that he was steering with one hand and holding a bottle of beer in the other. It was time to get social.

"Any beer left?" Marissa did her best to sound casual. But she would have pushed Ethan overboard if he had said no.

"Cooler's right up here. All the better to drink and drive." Ethan smiled encouragingly. He was the first person Marissa had approached all day. It was kind of flattering. What he didn't realize was that to Marissa, the beer was a lot more appealing than the boy.

Summer, meanwhile, had finally found someone who didn't grate on her. Ben wasn't the most fascinating guy, but he was oddly appealing. Up close, he was even a little cuter than she had given him credit for. He was the propman in his drama club.

"So, after trying a dozen antique stores and yard sales and Goodwills, you know where I finally found that mirror? In my grandmother's attic! And she made me pay for it!" Ben laughed, thrilled to have Summer's attention.

Summer's laughter stopped abruptly when she was hit with the crazy urge to grab Ben by the face and pull him in for a kiss. Where did that come from? He was nowhere near as hot as the other guys. And the whole propman thing wasn't exactly making her toes tingle.

So, what was it about him? It was not a difficult question to answer. The dark curly hair. The tall, lanky body. The dorky T-shirt. He was like a Seth understudy.

This is out of control. I need to erase Cohen from my memory. Like that surgery in Eternal Sunshine. *Why isn't that real? Why can't I do that? Why can't I convince my mind that Seth Cohen never happened?*

Two beers later and Marissa had taken over the steering. "Just keep it steady. You're doing a great job," Ethan reassured her.

Marissa didn't need his reassurance. "We have the ocean in California, too," she said, annoyed. "I *have* been sailing before."

Her irritation only amused Ethan. "Boy, and you

must have hated it. Because you probably had this big cargo of fish. And this humongous storm came out of nowhere. And everyone on your ship was killed, and you were the only survivor of a perfect storm, and you've hated sailing to this day."

He finally got a smile out of Marissa. Okay, maybe Summer was right. You throw these guys a little bone and it makes their day.

Ethan decided to press his luck. "There's this party tonight —"

Marissa cut him off. "I have plans."

"That's cool. There's pretty much a party happening every night this week." He opened a fresh bottle for Marissa.

Parties. Beer. Just what she would need to survive the week. She gave Ethan an encouraging smile. "I'll give you our number."

11

When Seth went back down to the studio after lunch to find Milla and get started with his job, she wasn't there. The only person around was a stagehand, hammering part of the set together, so Seth wandered over to him and waited until the guy looked up from his work to ask if he knew where the Cutters had gone.

"They're probably in their dressing room," the stagehand said disinterestedly. "Down the hall to the right."

"Thanks," Seth said. Then, because he couldn't resist sharing his good fortune: "I'm going to be Milla's assistant for the week she's here."

The stagehand snorted. "Good luck," he said, in a "better you than me" voice, and went back to his hammering.

Seth looked at him, surprised. Maybe he was misreading the guy's tone, and he really was simply wishing him luck. Or maybe, probably, the guy was jealous of Seth and trying to spoil it for him.

"Thanks," Seth said, and, shaking his head, walked down the hall toward the dressing rooms. The hall was painted with a mural of the MTV spaceman, and Jimi Hendrix was piping through the speakers. Marveling again at how cool his life had suddenly gotten, Seth stopped in front of a door with Milla's name on it, printed under a big gold star. He knocked, then held his breath until the door opened.

Milla was wearing a short, silky robe of the sort that would fuel Seth's fantasies for years to come, and high-heeled fuzzy mules straight out of a Ginger Rogers movie. Her hair was pulled up off her neck in a complicated knot, and her face, completely free of makeup, looked even more beautiful than Seth had ever imagined it. She looked young, at least younger than she did in her videos, and fragile, and when she saw Seth, her face moved into a dazzling smile.

"It's the boy with the cool shirt," she said in her heavy Scottish accent.

"Seth," he responded, holding out his hand to shake.

Her hand was cool in his, weighed down by the enormous jeweled rings that decorated every finger. "What can I do for you, Seth?"

"It's more like what can *I* do for *you*?" Seth answered.

Milla looked at him quizzically, so Seth hurried to explain. "I've been assigned to be your assistant for the week," he said. "So anything you need, anything at all —" He trailed off as her face darkened.

"You're my assistant?" she confirmed, and Seth nodded.

The smile left her face entirely, replaced by a dark scowl. "Then where the hell have you been?! It's"— glancing at a large watch that took up half her arm —"one o'clock! I haven't had my lunch yet, I need my outfit for tonight pressed, Mr. Pumpers needs a walk —"

"Mr. Pumpers?" Seth asked, then immediately wished he hadn't.

"Don't interrupt me!" Milla shouted. "How dare you! You are already the worst assistant I have ever had. Ever! After"— another look at the watch — "three minutes working for me."

She stared at him, her hands on her hips, and Seth looked down at the floor in horrified confusion, unsure what just happened to set this woman off.

"Well?" she demanded. "What do you have to say for yourself?"

"Um." Seth tried desperately to think of something to calm her rage. "I love your new CD."

Milla threw up her hands and turned on her heel. She stormed back into her dressing room and flounced down onto the couch. Seth waited in the doorway, unsure if he should follow her in or not.

"I'm waiting!" came the command. "And shut the door behind you."

Seth did as he was told, wondering briefly if it was too late to find Ryan and trade back.

* * *

Ryan, meanwhile, was sprawled on a bright red overstuffed couch in the fifth-floor screening room with a bunch of the other interns, watching videos. Marco had disappeared right after lunch, but all the other mailroom interns were there, including a girl named Tess who was slouched next to Ryan, her denim-covered thigh pressed against him.

Ryan didn't mind her invading his space. As a matter of fact, he would be happy to have her take up more of it. Tess was the cutest girl he'd seen in a long time; cute in that way he was learning was indigenous to New York — short black skirt, goofy thrift-store tee, impossibly high heels. Ryan wasn't sure how she was able to actually walk in those things, but as long as they kept her on the couch next to him, he wasn't going to ask to see a demonstration.

She'd introduced herself when she sat down, but they hadn't talked any more after that. Ryan wanted to, he was just waiting for a video to come on that she didn't pay attention to.

No telling when that would happen, though — Tess was riveted to the giant TV in the front of the room that was playing all the newest songs from the coolest bands. She bobbed her head and snapped her fingers along with the music, occasionally doing a little shimmy that Ryan found adorable. He didn't think she'd ever turn her attention to him . . . until Marco strode into the room and snapped the TV off.

"Back to work, people," Marco shouted over the groans and complaints of the lazing interns. "Mail won't deliver itself."

Everyone slowly pulled themselves to their feet, headed out of the screening room back down to the basement mailroom, and Ryan seized the opportunity to start a conversation with Tess.

"You think he's mad?" he asked in a low voice, gesturing at Marco with his chin.

Tess smiled and shook her head. "Naw, Marco's cool. Especially to the interns — I guess he thinks since they don't pay us, they shouldn't yell at us."

"Nice," Ryan said. He stepped aside to let her go through the doorway first, then caught up, walking beside her down to the mailroom.

"You a devil?" he asked.

She looked confused for a minute, then followed his gaze to her T-shirt: dark green cotton with MASSAPEQUA LI'L DEVILS printed across it in faded yellow letters. Tess shook her head.

"My little brother used to play peewee football."

"Me too," Ryan said. "I was a Tiger."

"I was a Devilette — a cheerleader," Tess informed him. She stopped in the hall and did a little cheer, unself-consciously kicking her leg up so high Ryan could — almost — get a peek of the pale strip of skin above the top of her thigh-high nylons. "P-S-Y-C-H-E-D! Psyched is what we wanna be! Get psyched! All right, all right, get psyched!"

She flung her arms out in a hurkee and looked at Ryan expectantly.

"Devil-*ettes*?" he said dryly.

Tess opened her mouth in an O of mock out-rage, then slugged Ryan hard on the shoulder. "Just for that, I'm not going to show you my splits."

She strode down the hall, then tossed back over her shoulder, "At least, not right now."

Ryan blinked — they didn't make girls like this in the O.C.! Then, before she could get away, he hurried after her.

While the job description of the mailroom sounded really boring, in practice, it was a lot of fun. The kids who worked there were all cool and, with the exception of a couple of overambitious film-school students, laid-back. Music played constantly, every-one joked and teased one another, and the few times he was sent to deliver a package to an office on another floor, he really enjoyed seeing how all the different departments were run.

So when a package arrived for Milla MacNeil, Ryan volunteered to take it to her. He was dying to see how Seth was enjoying his job and couldn't wait to tell him all about the fantastic girl he'd just met!

When the dressing room door had swung shut behind Seth, he was surprised at the wave of fear that had washed over him. He'd spend many furtive hours imagining this exact moment — him and Milla, *alone* together. Usually it elicited a rather

78

enjoyable response. So why now did he feel like a helpless beetle caught in a black widow's web?

"Did you want me to"— God, what had she said she needed done? —"order you some lunch?"

"No. I already did that myself." She stared silently at him, waiting.

Okay. "Sorry," he said, trying to look properly abashed.

"What you need to do is take Mr. Pumpers for his walk."

"Who is Mr. Pumpers?" Seth asked, looking around the room for whatever horrible yappy little purse-dog she brought on tour with her.

But Milla pointed, and a gigantic black mound that Seth had originally mistaken for a second couch rose to four stocky feet. "What the hell is that thing?" he asked, taking a step back.

"Mr. Pumpers is a Tosa." Off Seth's blank look: "A Japanese fighting mastiff."

That did not sound good. "Is that a *dog*?" he asked, taking another step back.

"Of course," she replied, scorn naked in her voice. "You aren't afraid of dogs, are you?"

Well, not exactly. Seth wasn't afraid of collies or golden retrievers, and when he was little he'd spent many Chrismukkahs begging his parents for a basset hound. But this thing. Mr. Pumpers. Yeah, Seth kinda *was* afraid.

"He needs to be walked for at least half an hour or he gets grouchy," Milla told Seth, snapping a leash onto the Tosa's collar and handing it to Seth. "And make sure to clean up after him. There's nothing worse than owners who don't take care of their pets."

Ignoring the irony, Seth opened the door and clucked his tongue at the gigantic dog. Instantly Mr. Pumpers was racing toward the exit, dragging Seth along behind him.

Three good things about walking the dog: 1. People, *girls*, stopped to scratch Mr. Pumpers' ears and ask Seth about the gigantic animal. 2. The walk from MTV to Bryant Park was really beautiful. Walking through midtown in the afternoon gave Seth an entirely different perspective of the city than he had hanging out in the Village the previous evening. In midtown, people were serious and rushed and seemed like they were all on their way to make important things happen. The air seemed to crackle with energy and ambition, and Seth again could envision himself making this city his home someday. And number three? Half an hour without being yelled at by Milla!

The sole downside? Cleaning up Mr. Pumpers' "business," a veritable mountain of odor. Seth held his nose and shut his eyes, and silently thanked his parents for never giving in to his request for a pet.

They walked until Seth was sure there was no grouchiness left in the dog. He let them both back into Milla's dressing room, then went to fill Mr. Pumpers' dish with fresh, cool water.

He'd just set the bowl down when there was a knock at the door and Ryan poked his head in.

"Hey!" Seth said, a drowning man seeing a life preserver.

"How's it going? Are you completely stoked?" Ryan asked. He handed the package to Seth and crossed the room, patting the dog, who was slobbering away at the water.

"It's going — um," Seth broke off as Milla walked in.

"What's happening in here?" she demanded.

"You got a package," Seth told her, but she wasn't paying attention. She strode across the room and picked up her dog's water dish.

"Is this *tap water*?" she asked.

Seth shot a pleading glance at Ryan, then nodded. "He was thirsty, so I —"

"He only drinks Evian, you idiot boy!" she shouted, and threw the bowl at Seth.

It missed, clanging against wall behind him, but the spray of falling water soaked Seth's shirt and jeans.

Seth looked down at his dripping clothes in disbelief, then turned to Ryan. "It's going great!"

12

Funny how getting ready to go out to dinner with her dad reminded Marissa of preparing for a date. Would they run out of things to talk about? Would he think she was dull? Was he going to be racing through the night to get it over with? Did she look her best?

A lot more nerve-wracking, actually.

Because when a date went wrong, usually both people were happy to never see each other again, and life went on. Even when you broke up with someone you really cared about, life went on. But if Jimmy were ever to stop loving her, then Marissa probably *would* need to be put in an asylum. Jimmy felt like the last good solid certainty in her life. She couldn't lose him.

Dinner was at a glorified fish shack, but Marissa didn't mind. It was cozy and Jimmy had brought her because it was one of his favorite places. She knew that after she was back home, it would be kind of cool to picture exactly where he might be eating that night.

"A little warning about the crab cakes. They will spoil you for all other crab cakes for the remainder of your life. Are you prepared to make that kind of decision?" Jimmy teased.

"Is this the Velveeta-to-Brie theory of fine dining?" Marissa smiled. It was an old argument.

"Your mother always said give children the best life has to offer and they'll cultivate discriminating taste buds from an early age. But I always said start them off with the cheap stuff. By their teens, introduce them to a fairly good B-level of cuisine. But no one should taste the superlative stuff until they're past thirty. Your enjoyment of the mediocre food that comprises most of life's offerings will be ruined forever."

It felt like things between Marissa and Jimmy were back to the way they used to be. Back to the good days.

"Every once in a while, you just have to throw caution to the wind," Marissa responded.

Jimmy flagged the waitress down. "Waitress. Crab cakes!"

The waitress was a little surprised by Jimmy's exuberance, but this was clearly a carefree family outing.

"So, Mom was asked to do this huge design job. At some corporate law office. She's really excited," Marissa said offhandedly. Maybe Jimmy would be happy to hear that Julie was pulling her life together. But he just shrugged.

"Of course she's happy," Jimmy said with his

head down, not looking at Marissa. "There's a big check in it for her, and that's always been the most important thing to her. Morgan is also a really talented decorator, as you can tell from the house, but it's really something that pours out of her heart and soul. She'll never need to try and make money out of it."

Marissa bristled in response. "There's nothing wrong with trying to make a living."

"Of course not. I'm just impressed with Morgan's priorities. I'm really proud of her."

Marissa had to shove the conversation in a new direction immediately. "We have to sign up for fall classes pretty soon after we get back. I've never really been able to do the advanced computer stuff. But it might be good to know. I should probably take one of those classes for an elective."

Jimmy nodded enthusiastically. "You should talk to Kyle. He's a computer whiz. He can steer you toward the best classes; he knows all the programs inside out. He's very impressive."

Marissa leaned back in her seat, arms folded, scowling. "And wait, don't tell me. You're so proud of *him*, too."

Jimmy was blindsided by Marissa's change of mood. "What did I say?" he asked.

"Morgan this! Kyle that! Morgan that! Kyle this! I'm really getting sick of them. Why can't I have just one evening free from them? That's all I wanted. I didn't choose to have them in my life. Why do they keep getting dragged into my every waking moment?"

Jimmy was dumbfounded. He had noticed Marissa's silence that first night, and he had certainly seen earlier that morning that she wasn't into hanging out with Kyle. But he really expected that after an afternoon together, they would find some common ground. They were both smart, attractive, sweet kids.

"Morgan and Kyle are good people. From what I've seen, they've both been very welcoming to you."

"Welcoming? What are they welcoming me to? This is your home. And by extension, it's more my home than theirs. They have no right to welcome me into your home."

Clearly, Marissa had gone off the deep end. Jimmy did his best to deflect this tirade.

"Marissa, this woman has become an important part of my life. I can't even begin to tell you what a miracle it feels like to have found her. And I hate to see you upset, but you've gotta find some way to accept this."

Marissa had finally gotten her feelings out and she wasn't willing to give an inch. "I'm entitled to my opinion," she said.

"Are you? Was your mother entitled to hate Ryan as much as she did? And to do everything she could to keep the two of you apart? Even though you loved him? And you made each other happy?"

Surely Marissa would be able to see that she was being as blindly judgmental and as unfair as Julie had been with Ryan. But the similarities were lost on her. Ryan had never posed a threat to the way she felt about her father. "It's a totally different situation. Mom was . . . she was . . ."

Jimmy interjected, "She was wrong, Marissa. She was wrong." It was obvious that he believed the same was true of her.

To Marissa, it was the first definitive showdown with her absent rivals. And her father had clearly chosen sides.

The ride back home was deathly silent. Some mindless speculation about whether Summer enjoyed the luau. More suggestions for sightseeing, Jimmy stumbling on occasion to avoid mentioning that a particular recommendation came from Morgan. Marissa prayed that Summer was back at the house. She really needed to talk to someone.

The sight of Summer and Kyle laughing and relaxing on the front porch was understandably not a welcome one for Marissa. But it was a little hard for Jimmy as well. This was exactly what he had envisioned for Marissa and Kyle. Hitting it off, goofing around on the porch. The thought of a romantic complication had even crossed his mind briefly.

No danger of that, though.

"Jimmy, Mom's inside waiting for you," Kyle reminded him.

Jimmy did his best not to look at Marissa, knowing how she would take this news. After he went into the house, Summer scooted over on the couch. "Sit down, Coop. You have to hear about this luau. It was wild. You have to go to one before we leave."

Marissa backed away toward the door. "I'm kind of tired. I'll see you inside." A very terse nod to Kyle, and Marissa disappeared into the house.

This was probably the best opportunity Kyle would have to figure out what was going on. "You and Marissa are pretty tight, right?"

"BFF. Even when she's behaving like a jackass," Summer admitted with a wry smile.

Kyle was glad to hear that he was not the only one who had noticed that Marissa's behavior was a little extreme. "What's going on with her? I mean, I know the divorce is pretty recent and everything."

Summer thought for a minute. How to explain Marissa's sweet side to someone who would probably never see it? "You know that old Chinese curse 'May you live in interesting times'?" Well, last year was just a little too damn interesting for Coop. She really got put through the ringer. And I've done my best to cut her quite a bit of slack lately."

"Sure," Kyle responded.

"However"— Summer stood up —"even I have my limits." She slammed the door on her way into the house.

Kyle couldn't resist a grin. Someone needed to set Marissa straight, and Summer was definitely from the "take no prisoners" school.

* * *

Summer came into Marissa's bedroom to find her friend waiting impatiently. "First Mom and Luke. Now Dad and Morgan. You wouldn't happen to want to trade parents for the next two years, would you?"

But it was clear from the look on Summer's face that she wasn't going to be the sympathetic ear that Marissa needed.

"What? Marissa asked, annoyed.

Summer paced the room. "The what is that you have actually managed to make spring break in Buffalo seem like a missed opportunity. Luaus and sailing and buff semiclad male bodies — there may be more to life, but there's not much more to vacation. You even got some time alone with your dad tonight. And that still isn't enough for you?"

Summer was Marissa's final hope that someone else could see what was really going on. "No, as a matter of fact. I couldn't enjoy dinner with my dad. He kept going on and on about Morgan and Kyle and how I would just love them if I only gave them a chance."

"Coop, Kyle is the best combination of brains and body this side of the Pacific. What's not to love? I mean, seriously fun. It's not like you have to jump his bones. 'Cause that actually might be a little incestuous."

Marissa grimaced. "Do not even think about me and Kyle being in the same family. Ditto for Morgan. I am not letting these people steal away any more of my life than they already have."

Summer could see that Marissa was beyond reason but took one last stab. "No one has stolen anything from you. Morgan's really okay. Sure, she's a little bit *Stepford,* but in a good way."

Marissa got the same sinking feeling that she had at the end of dinner with Jimmy. "No one is on my side," she grumbled.

"Yeah," Summer said, backing out of the room, "what does that tell you?"

13

"She's ruining my perfect vacation," Seth complained. He took a sip of the Manhattan he'd ordered from the hotel bartender and grimaced. Nasty stuff. Now he was sorry they hadn't carded him.

"It's not ruined — it's been one day." Ryan clapped Seth sympathetically on the back and shoved his Coke in front of Seth, who took a huge gulp to try and wash the taste of the whiskey out of his mouth.

"You don't understand," Seth continued after he swallowed. "She's a monster. A monster! She ordered me around like a slave, she never once said thank you, you saw her throw that water on me!"

"Yeah, that was rough," said Ryan, trying not to laugh. He didn't quite pull it off, though, because Seth noticed the corners of his mouth twitching and straightened on his bar stool indignantly.

"It's not funny!"

"I know," Ryan said contritely.

"She wouldn't let me change out of my wet

clothes." Seth looked flustered at the memory. "I *chafed*."

"That sucks," Ryan agreed.

"Their new CD isn't even any good," Seth added. He took another mouthful of the Manhattan and swallowed, coughing. "This was supposed to be the best week ever, and now look at it."

"It can still be a great week," Ryan told him, but Seth shook his head.

"Nope. It's spoiled. Nothing can save it now." He peeked out of the corner of his eye at Ryan, then shook his head dolefully. "Nothing, except . . ."

"What?"

Seth looked at Ryan, then quickly away. "Switch back with me."

"What?!"

"Switch back with me. I'll work in the mailroom like I was supposed to, and you can be Milla's assistant."

"Are you crazy?" Ryan asked, laughing. "No way am I switching with you."

"But you'd be so much better at it than I am," Seth pleaded. "What the hell do I know about working with bands? All I do at The Bait Shop is mop up after someone pukes."

"Well, that's good practice for when Mr. Pumpers gets a hairball."

"Dogs don't get hairballs," Seth told him.

"See? I didn't know that. You really are the perfect assistant for Milla."

Seth grouchily took another swallow of whiskey,

then spit it back in his glass. "God, why do I keep drinking that? It's terrible."

"You're a glutton for punishment," Ryan said. "Which is why working for the Cutters is perfect for you."

"I just really think Dad's friend Robert assigned us to those positions for a reason —" Seth started, but Ryan held up a hand to cut him off.

"Seth. Stop. I'm not going to change jobs with you."

"Why not?" Seth whined.

"Even if I wanted to — WHICH I DON'T — I have an added incentive for working in the mailroom."

Seth lifted his head from where it was resting on the bar in despair and looked at his friend.

"What? Do they give you free CDs? All the pizza you can eat? You get to be background dancers in the videos? What?"

"Tess," Ryan said simply.

"Tess?" Seth repeated. "What's Tess? A new band?"

"Uh-uh," Ryan said, unable to keep a smile from stretching across his face. "Tess is a girl. *The* girl."

"Reeeeeally," Seth said, stretching the word out lasciviously.

Ryan nodded. "She's just — cool, you know? Like, I get her, and she gets me. Right away."

"Wow." Seth nodded approvingly. "So tell me about her. What's she like?"

"Well, she used to be a cheerleader, and she has a brother, and —" Ryan thought hard, then realized that was basically all he knew about her. "— and her name is Tess," he finished somewhat lamely.

But Seth chose the high ground and held out a palm for Ryan to slap. "Sounds good. I happened to meet a girl myself."

Ryan cocked an eyebrow. "Milla?"

"No," Seth said. "Leah."

Ryan looked at him blankly for a second, then blinked.

"That weird girl from lunch?"

"She's not weird," Seth said. "She's just misunderstood."

"You're right. I'm sorry," Ryan said, genuinely meaning it. Although it had been a long time since Seth was considered an outcast in Newport Beach, Ryan was sensitive to any reference that would remind Seth of his former friendless state. Sometimes it was hard to censor himself because he never thought of Seth as being anything other than cool and alternative. If he thought about it, he figured that that was about the best compliment he could give Seth — not even noticing his residual geekiness. But in any case, he didn't want to do anything to make Seth feel bad about himself.

"So you talked to Leah after the rest of us left?"

Seth nodded. "She's really nice."

"So's Tess."

"Well, here's to scoring in New York," Seth said impishly, raising his drink. He and Ryan clinked glasses in a toast, then drank.

"Jesus!" Seth said, spitting out the Manhattan again. Having finally learned his lesson, he pushed the glass across the bar away from him, then motioned to the bartender to bring him a Coke.

"Here's to *love* in New York," Ryan corrected, and Seth smiled.

"I'll drink to that!"

14

Jimmy had said that he took the whole week off from work so that he could spend more time with Marissa. But some kind of "emergency" pulled him back in for the day. Marissa suspected that he jumped on the flimsiest opportunity to avoid her that day. After last night, what was there left to say?

So, Marissa was stuck with Kyle's sailboat crowd again. More girls this time. And more space . . . they were sprawled on blankets on Ulua Beach, soaking up the sun and enjoying the warm spring day. Marissa had seriously considered just staying at the house, but it was wall-to-wall reminders of Morgan's presence. Even the smell of homemade oatmeal raisin cookies in the air was an intrusion.

Summer was having the time of her life. Several boys were team-teaching her to surf. It seemed to involve an awful lot of land drills, with Summer lying on a board on the sand and then leaping up on it. It was unclear as to whether or not she was ever going to actually make it into the water that day. But she was having so much fun that Marissa truly envied her. Still, Marissa felt too cut off from the world to even make the attempt to reach out.

She had remembered her iPod this time. There was no better signal that she wanted to be left alone. She listened to a mix of songs that Ryan once put together for her. She had felt foolish even bringing it, but now it felt like her final lifeline. In their best times, Ryan stood by her through everything. If they were still together, then none of this would be hurting so badly. It was a pretty feeble thing to cling to, but it felt like all she had left.

No. No. No. No. No. If Marissa knew that someone hated her, there was no way that she would constantly be getting in their face. So why was Kyle strolling in her direction with a big smile on his face? A victory smile, apparently. He must have known that he had captured the loyalty of everyone who should have been in Marissa's corner. *Let the gloating commence.*

"Whatcha listening to?" Kyle inquired loudly. Marissa pulled her earplugs out reluctantly.

"Nothing. Music. Different stuff. What do you want?"

Kyle knew exactly what to expect from Marissa now. He knew better than to get upset. "I was just remembering. You and I never got around to that horseback ride. I was thinking, maybe tomorrow?"

What was his problem? It was a big island and there was no reason for them to interact outside of Dad's house. "Sorry, Kyle. I'm pretty sure I have laundry plans."

Kyle was undeterred. He had pretty much figured that if he got Marissa to agree to this at all, then it would take, minimum, a good twenty minutes of arm twisting.

"Pull something out of the laundry basket. The horse won't mind."

Marissa was amazed. "You know what my answer is. Are you a sadist or a masochist?"

Kyle cocked his head thoughtfully. "You know, I never gave the matter much thought. Am I inflicting any pain or discomfort?" From Marissa's expression, absolutely. "I must be a sadist, then — good to know."

"Why? Why do you keep asking? Why do you keep trying this . . . friendly thing?"

Kyle got to his feet and knocked the sand off his legs. "I keep trying for the same reason that you should say yes. Because it would make your father really happy."

The implication was that Kyle cared more about Jimmy's happiness than Marissa did!? *How dare he?*

Later, when Kyle dropped them off at the house, Marissa muttered a thank you without even looking at him.

"So, we'll be back in about two hours for dinner. Mom and I were thinking, maybe Chinese?" Kyle either didn't notice or did his best to ignore the look of disgust on Marissa's face. His car rolled back down the driveway.

"Dad didn't say anything about having dinner with them tonight," Marissa wailed.

"Well, it's probably because we all know how you love a good surprise," Summer responded with a smirk. "Actually, it's the Get Marissa Cooper to Grow Up Island Conspiracy, and we are *all* in on it."

Marissa stomped into the house, straight up to her father in the kitchen. "Dad, why can't the three of us just have a quiet dinner? Why do they have to be part of every single evening? They can have dinner with you every day next week. And the week after that. And the week after that. And all of May. And all of June. And eleven months out of the year. Why can't they just give us this week together? Why is that so much to ask?"

Jimmy had known this was coming. Just as all parents have to deal with their babies' screaming when they're not allowed to play with shiny knives and colorful pills, Jimmy knew that being a good father on that particular day meant *not* giving in to Marissa.

"*They* are coming because they want to get to know you and they only have the very limited window of this week to do that. In any case, the plans have already been made. And I would certainly love for you to join us," Jimmy said quietly.

Marissa's mind was spinning. Join *them!* She raged inside. *It should be them joining us! I am not the third wheel.*

"I'm really not in the mood for a big group dinner. I'm just going to grab a bite and get some shopping done," Marissa informed him.

Jimmy nodded sadly. It was out of his hands.

Marissa stormed out of the kitchen to find Summer standing at the door, eavesdropping. "All right, Coop. It's you and me, then."

Marissa sighed with relief. She wasn't going to be totally abandoned.

"Don't get all misty. I just haven't gotten my shopping quota in this week."

Half an hour into their shopping trip and Summer was already regretting her decision. Marissa could not believe that Jimmy had really gone to dinner without her, and for someone who didn't like Morgan and Kyle, she wouldn't stop talking about them. "What the hell am I even doing here if he has absolutely zero interest in spending any time with me?" Marissa ranted.

"Might I suggest salvaging this trip with a couple of new dresses?" Summer suggested. "And you also promised to help me decide on the bikinis. Orange or blue?"

The shops at Wailea may have been a little touristy, but they were still Summer's idea of a good time. There were none of the chain stores you found at every shopping center in the continental U.S. — no Gaps or J. Crews or Banana Republics. Instead, Wailea boasted rows of tiny storefronts, filled with some of the most wonderful clothes Summer and Marissa had ever seen. Cotton dresses as light as air, a stack of bikinis so colorful they looked like a flock of exotic birds roosting on the shelf, baby-doll tees with Hawaiian phrases stretching across the front. Novelty grass skirts and hand-tooled leather sandals and shell-encrusted camisoles. A rack with a greater variety of sunglasses than the girls had ever seen at the trendiest boutique in L.A.

They wandered into every single shop on the strip, mingling with hundreds of tourists bogged down with leis and broad-brimmed straw hats, sultry native shopgirls and small boys trading Polaroids for dollar bills. They looked at thousands of items of clothing, tried on hundreds, and bought as many as their credit cards would support.

But as much fun as the shopping was, Marissa could not be distracted. "I need to call the airline first thing in the morning. I need to get my ticket changed. Why should I stay here another day?"

Summer tried to swallow her exasperation. "Oh, so many reasons. Including the fact that you have a guest. That would be *moi*. Second reason, as if we needed one, is the possibility that this mental condition of yours is going to clear up. Like a twenty-four-hour flu. You'll just wake up tomorrow and be a totally normal, rational Marissa. I know it's a long shot, but I really have to pin my hopes on something."

On the street, Marissa flagged down a taxi. "I'm sorry. You stay a while and finish up the shopping. I just need to clear my head. I just need a little time alone."

Summer shrugged, resigned. "Are you going straight home?" she asked Marissa.

"No," Marissa said carefully, "I think I'm going to go for a walk."

Summer didn't like the sound of that. "You're going to go home and then you're going to go for a walk?"

Marissa wouldn't meet Summer's eye. "I'll see you later. Okay?" Marissa stepped in the taxi, and Summer watched pensively as it drove off.

Marissa hadn't mentioned to Summer that Ethan had given her the address of a big party that night. Summer was almost as bad as Marissa's parents about worrying that she was drinking too much. If ever Marissa needed to relax and forget, then that was definitely the night.

The party was packed. A spring break blowout. It took over an hour before Marissa even spotted Ethan. Of course, he was really not the reason she came. By the time they ran into each other, Marissa was on her fourth beer.

15

"Ham and swiss on rye with mustard, tuna with light mayo, lettuce, and bacon on a croissant, two cheese knishes, two turkey clubs, one toasted, one not, and a reuben, hold the kraut, on pumpernickel," Seth read off the scrap of paper where he'd written down the band's lunch orders.

"Not a reuben," the gruff oldster behind the counter at the deli barked.

Seth double-checked his list. "Uh — no, I want a reuben, no sauerkraut, on pumpernickel. Please."

"If there's no kraut, it's not a reuben," the counterman insisted.

Seth sighed. It was only lunchtime, but already he felt like the day had been going on forever. First Milla had yelled at him for being late. Then she was mad that he hadn't known to set up a little tray of snacks backstage while she was recording her guest VJ spots. Then he got on her nerves with, as she put it, his creepy noisy breathing, and when he told her he'd be happy to stop breathing except then she'd have to actually do the work of dialing 911 herself, she sent him out to fetch sandwiches for the band. But of course even that had to be a big freaking pain-in-the-ass, since apparently there was no such thing as a krautless reuben.

"Fine, I'll just take a corned beef with — what is it, swiss and Russian dressing on pumpernickel."

"That it?" the counterman asked, scrawling Seth's order on a pad.

"Yeah," Seth started, then realized he hadn't ordered anything for himself. If he was going to deal with Milla for five more hours, he needed to keep his strength up. "Wait, no —" he said, and the counter guy scowled as several people behind Seth in line groaned.

"I also want a —" he scanned the menu board above the guy's head. "— roast beef on whole wheat with extra horseradish."

The man took Seth's money, then gestured for him to have a seat while he waited for his sandwiches to be ready.

Seth perched on the edge of one of the worn wooden chairs. He didn't allow himself to get too comfortable, because if he did, he knew he'd never manage to force himself to go back to work.

But before he knew it, the man was piling the sandwiches into a brown paper sack, throwing handfuls of sour dill pickles and napkins and salt and pepper packets on top, and handing the entire thing to Seth.

Seth hefted the bag into his arms, but as he

turned away from the counter, who should come in but Ryan and the other interns!

There were six or seven kids with Ryan, and altogether they formed a happy, noisy, laughing group. They shoved together two of the largest tables in the place, draping backpacks over chairs and snatching up menus.

Ryan saw Seth and grinned. "Hey! Perfect timing," he said. "Grab a chair and join us."

"I can't," Seth said, his mood growing even darker. He held up the paper bag and grimaced. "Milla has low blood sugar."

A girl sitting at the table overheard him and laughed, and walked up behind Ryan. It was Tess. She slipped one arm through Ryan's, and held her other hand out for Seth to shake.

"You must be Seth," she said. "I'm Tess. Ryan was telling me how you got trapped into working for the wicked witch of the east."

"Wasn't that the one who got smooshed by the house?" Ryan asked.

"I wish," Seth said. "Nice to meet you, Tess, but if I don't get her highness her lunch right away, not even the wizard will be able to save me."

He trudged out the door and Ryan and Tess looked at each other.

"Poor guy," Tess said, and Ryan nodded.

"Yeah, but better him than me!"

Tess laughed and tilted her head back to look up into Ryan's eyes. "How bout if for lunch, I pick your sandwich for you, and you pick my sandwich for me."

"Okay," Ryan said. "But what if we don't like what the other person picked?"

"Too bad," Tess said. "You have to eat it anyway."

"Well, are you going to order me something gross, like tongue or chicken liver?"

Tess shook her head. "Guess you just have to trust me." She sashayed up to the counter and said something to the counterman, then walked back to Ryan. "Same as I have to trust you," she said.

Ryan grinned. Again he was struck by how much he liked this girl. She was so easy-going and confident. Was it because she was a New Yorker? Because he didn't know *any* girls as self-assured as Tess at home — either in Newport Beach or Chino. All the girls in California were so worried about carbs and calories and how they looked in their Juicy Couture that there's no way they'd risk having someone order a patty melt or something fattening like that for them. Actually —

"One patty melt, please," Ryan told the counter man, and smiled. He just hoped Tess had ordered him something good as well.

When Seth got back to the studio, he wished he'd stayed away for good. Milla was happy enough to get her not-a-reuben, but when Seth sat down to eat his own lunch, she gave him a look of such incredulity that he actually glanced around to see what freakish spectacle was behind him.

"What do you think you're doing?" she asked, her honeyed voice hard and unpleasant.

Seth glanced down at his sandwich. Wasn't it obvious? "I'm *eating*," he said, carefully enunciating each syllable.

Milla's voice grew even more disbelieving. "You don't have time to eat."

"Why not?"

In response, Milla shoved a piece of paper at him. Seth looked down at it — it was a list of errands she wanted him to do for her.

Seth quickly scanned the list. "Pick up dry cleaning," was first, followed by "make dinner reservations," "clean dressing room," "pick up driver's license renewal forms," "mail out birthday package to mother," "research cell phone company plans for better rates," and about a million more stupid, boring, personal errands. There was nothing on the list that had anything remotely to do with music, and, frankly, if Seth wanted to spend his vacation standing in line at the DMV, he could have stayed in the O.C.

"What are you waiting for?" Milla asked.

Seth jumped up, shoved his uneaten sandwich in his pocket, and whistled for Milla's dog. "Mr. Pumpers is starting to look grumpy," he said, and snapping the leash on him, made his escape.

Tess had ordered Ryan the house special; a sandwich called the Metropolitan, which was turkey, bacon, and cheese, heated on the grill and then doused with gravy. Ryan thought it was a very good choice indeed.

But when he set her patty melt down in front of her, Tess looked down at it with a dismayed expression.

Inwardly Ryan groaned. Now it was going to come out — Tess was one of those girls who thought that beef was fattening, or who wouldn't eat bread after ten AM or something ridiculous like that, that would make her exactly the same as all the girls he knew at home. But when he asked her what was wrong, she gave a little shrug.

"This has onions on it," she told him.

"You don't like onions?" he asked. But Tess just smiled a crooked little smile.

"I like them fine. It's just — if I eat onions, then we can't kiss later."

Ryan matched her smile with one of his own. "Then — I guess we better kiss now."

"Good idea," Tess said softly, leaning in.

Ryan's mouth met hers, and as he closed his eyes and parted his lips, he marveled once again at what a different and wonderful kind of girl Tess was.

16

Ethan's party was in a three-story house and it was crammed to full capacity. Mostly college kids, but Marissa felt confident that she blended in. The tight feeling in her chest melted away. It was such a wonderful relief to be somewhere where no one really knew her or had any expectations of her. And no one could disappoint her. A clean slate for one blissful evening.

The college boys were very accommodating. Marissa had a drink in hand and was soon surrounded by an instant fan club on a long sofa in the front room. "You been diving yet?" one of them asked. "Oh, you can't leave without checking out these waters. I can show you where to get some really cheap equipment. How about tomorrow? Got any plans for tomorrow?"

The thought of removing herself from the Dad-Morgan-Kyle situation was an irresistible temptation. Marissa definitely wanted to keep that option open. "That sounds great. I can't make any plans for sure yet. But I'll keep it in mind. Why don't you take my number? It's 949 . . ."

Marissa laughed as not only her prospective diving partner scrambled for a pen but so did about half a dozen guys within earshot.

This level of popularity was pretty exhilarating. Oh, Marissa had always been considered one of the cool kids at school. When she was dating Luke, they were one of the golden couples of Harbor High.

But then they broke up, which was a strike against her.

Then she started seeing Ryan, who everyone just assumed was a thug from Chino with a terrible reputation. Marissa's social status had definitely taken a tumble over that.

Not that she had any regrets. Being with Ryan for even that short time had been so intense, so amazing. But it was over now, and it had left her a little adrift in the school hierarchy. Having a group of boys jostling for her attention right now was the antidote to what was becoming a long, stressful week.

It was in the long line for the bathroom that she finally spotted Ethan. Marissa had completely for-gotten about him by that time. In fact, if she hadn't run into him, she never would have given him a sec-ond thought. But there he was, and, after all, he was the one who had invited her. They hugged like old friends.

"Marissa, I'm so glad you could make it," Ethan gushed. Clearly, the beer he was holding was not his first. "We've got a lot of cool stuff in this house. Let me show you around." Marissa had been wanting to check out the rest of the house, so she quickly agreed.

There was something going on in every room. There was a pool table and dartboards. Old-fashioned video arcade games. Ping-Pong table. Poker table. Swimming pool in the back. As well as some very heavy breathing going on behind several locked doors. It was a college utopia.

Ethan introduced Marissa to dozens of people. A lot of them assumed that she was Ethan's new girlfriend. But that was kind of fun. It made Marissa happy to imagine that in a couple of years, she was going to be out on her own, and her life was going to be free and full of fun times and nights like this. Also, Ethan was so much cuter than she had remembered. That is, she had noticed on the sailboat that he was a good-looking guy, but it just wasn't impressing her at the time.

He was being so sweet, too. Trying to make sure she felt at home. Running downstairs and getting more cold beer for her. That was one thing that Ethan had quickly picked up on during their sail: Marissa should never be without a beer.

That's so funny. That girl looks just like Summer. Marissa realized that she was getting a little woozy, and seeing Summer's look-alike confirmed it. She was definitely buzzed. It was a fantastic sensation. Like coming home to a warm, cozy, safe place.

But Marissa's restful state of mind was soon dashed. That wasn't just a girl who looked like Summer. It was, in fact, a very tired, very angry Summer, who had just spent twenty minutes roving through the house looking for Marissa.

Ethan was thrilled. He had invited Summer to the party that afternoon. She had declined, saying that she already had plans.

"Summer, it is so cool to see you. Marissa said that you weren't feeling well."

Summer scowled at Marissa. "I did have a sick feeling in the pit of my stomach earlier. At first I thought it was the flu. But then it just turned out to be a good hunch."

Marissa looked away. Why did she have to deal with a guilt trip right then? Just when she was starting to feel good again.

Ethan held a beer out to Summer. "Can I get you anything to drink?"

"Yeah. Coffee. A little cream, a little sugar," Summer answered.

"Whatever you say." Ethan headed back downstairs.

Marissa sized Summer up hopefully. Maybe she could pull her into the party mood. "That coffee is going to keep you up all night. You should try something a little more relaxing."

"The coffee is for you," Summer responded. "And then we're getting out of here. We have a little leeway because I left a bogus note for your dad saying that we were seeing a midnight movie. But that still means we need to get home pronto."

Was she kidding? Marissa had been basking in newfound sensations of freedom and independence and glorious impending adulthood. She was not about to let anyone order her around tonight.

"I'm not going anywhere. I'm having a good time. And I'm staying. All night if I want to."

Summer pointed to the beer in Marissa's hand. "How many of those have you had?"

Six, but that really wasn't any of Summer's business.

Summer hooked her arm around Marissa's and tried to pull her toward the door. "C'mon. Let's go downstairs while you can still handle stairs."

Marissa pushed Summer away. "Leave me alone. You can stay or you can go. I really don't care. But just leave me alone," Marissa said, retreating to an armchair across the room.

Summer looked around in frustration. Drunken guys were everywhere. There was no telling how quickly things might get out of control. Summer pulled out her cell phone and dialed.

Now Marissa was in a bad mood. Summer, her parents, Ryan. Why were they always harping about a little harmless drinking? Everyone was so quick to assume that Marissa had a problem. Even to the point of threatening to send her back to some creepy therapist or an institution where she could "work on her issues in a warm, supportive environment." At least that's what the brochure had said. *I'm not an alcoholic,* Marissa thought. *I just wish everyone would leave me alone.* No matter what anyone said to her, Marissa had decided she wouldn't listen. Lies and humiliation — that's all it was. She was fine . . . even if her chair did suddenly feel like it was swaying.

By the time Ethan got back to Marissa, she was feeling hot and drowsy. "I need a little bit of fresh air," she muttered.

"I know what you need!" Ethan said excitedly. "A dip in the pool. It'll perk you right up. And there's a Jacuzzi attached. You'll love it."

Marissa didn't take much convincing. A cool swim sounded perfect.

She was already down by the pool when she remembered one critical thing. "I don't have a swimsuit."

Ethan immediately stripped down to his boxer shorts. "Swimsuits. Underwear. They're the exact same thing. Really. They're just marketed differently and sold in different departments. But they're identical and functionally interchangeable. Trust me."

It made sense. Or at least, the water looked so inviting that Marissa was dying for an excuse to get in. She slipped her clothes off to murmurs of appreciation and a small burst of applause from the guys around the pool.

Marissa leaped in with a splash and there was a quick scramble as several guys decided that it really was a good time for a swim.

Half an hour later, Marissa was nodding off in the Jacuzzi, arms folded over her chest. Her bra had disappeared some time ago. One of the boys had unhooked it when she'd splashed by him. It was annoying, but Ethan had promised to get her something to put on before she left the pool.

Where had he gone, anyway?

Eventually the pool had gotten too cold, and Marissa rolled over into the warm Jacuzzi. The bubbling water hid her toplessness and she felt totally comfortable again. So comfortable that she started nodding off. A few boys pointed at her, trying to decide who should help her out, and exactly whose bedroom she should recuperate in.

Marissa felt two strong arms encircle her waist and lift her out of the water. She yelled in angry protest and whirled around angrily to face . . . Kyle!

Her shock was quickly replaced by embarrassment when she remembered the missing bra. But Kyle had a coat ready to throw over her. He pushed Marissa toward the exit, past Summer, who followed grimly behind.

Between the two of them, Summer and Kyle managed to get Marissa safely back home and into her own bed.

Kyle left as quietly as he could. He was pretty shaken up. Yesterday, Marissa's problems had felt like Marissa's problems, and he was really only an innocent bystander in whatever was going on with her. But now he knew how big a part of the problem he was. He still remembered her last words to him at the door.

"My dad's not even going to miss me when I leave. Why should he? You can be the great kid that he always wanted. You two can be the perfect family that we never were."

Kyle stood frozen on the stairs a long time after Summer had helped Marissa stumble into the house. This wasn't just a routine divorce trauma. This was really, *really* bad.

17

"There you are," Seth said, running to catch up with Leah.

When she saw him, she blushed, the deep red spreading all the way to her ears, and gave Seth a little wave.

"Where've you been hiding?" Seth asked her. "I've been looking all over for you."

"Really?" Leah asked, the blush growing darker. "I've been around."

"Well, I'm glad I found you now. What're you up to?"

"I was going to run down to Starbucks and grab some coffee —" She hesitated, looking down at her feet, then blurted out, "Do you want to come?"

Seth's mind flashed to all the errands he still needed to run for Milla, then took less than a split second to decide to blow them off. "Absolutely," he said, and pressed the button for the elevator.

At the coffee shop, Seth was amazed at the amount of sugar and candy one girl could put in a cup. Leah ordered a caramel mocha latte with vanilla syrup and three sugars. It made Seth's teeth ache just watching her sip it.

"How are you liking working here?" Leah asked.

"Not so much," Seth answered. "It's really been a disappointment. Milla MacNeil is such a witch, I don't even like her band's music anymore," he said. In a rush, all of the humiliation and anger he'd suppressed during the past few days came tumbling out.

"She's such a bitter, self-involved, nasty person," he said, after running through the diatribe of all the injustices she'd piled on him over the last few days. "I don't understand why anybody would act that way."

"That sucks," Leah agreed. "Maybe you can ask Marco to switch you to a different department. We're looking for more people in accounting. It's boring, but maybe it wouldn't be so bad if both of us were there."

"It's too late," Seth said, fresh disappointment settling over him. "Tomorrow's my last day here, then we're headed back to California."

"Thank god," said a drawling voice behind them.

Seth turned — Milla had come into the coffee shop and was standing behind him, holding a cappuccino and eavesdropping.

"Young love, unrequited," she smirked. "It's the saddest story in the book. I might have to write a song about it."

117

Leah was blushing again. She sank back into the pillows on her chair like she was hoping to disappear right through them. Seth looked from her to Milla's tight, smug smile and pushed his chair back with a clatter, standing up and facing his tormentor.

"Why are you so awful?" he asked her.

"Maybe because I haven't had my coffee yet," she said, holding up her cup. "By the way, nice of you to offer to bring me back some, *assistant.*"

"I — I —" Seth was speechless. He could think of about a thousand nasty names to call her, but that would just be stooping to her level. He needed the perfect cutting remark that would make her think long and hard about treating people this way in the future, but words were failing him.

"I — I —" Milla mocked him. "Come on, let's go, break's over. Lots for you to do before you leave tomorrow."

Finally Seth thought of something to say. "No."

"No?"

"No," he repeated. "Leah's not done with her coffee, and I'm not leaving until —"

"I'm done," Leah said quickly, scrambling out of her chair. "And I really should be getting back to work, too. So — bye." And in a flash she was out the door.

Dismayed, Seth watched her leave, then turned to find Milla looking at him with one raised eyebrow. "Guess you're ready to get back to work now."

* * *

Milla kept a watchful eye on Seth, so it wasn't until a couple of hours later that he finally managed to slip away. He wanted to find Leah, but before that, he wanted to check in with Ryan and get his perspective.

He headed down to the mailroom and was struck again by the relaxed camaraderie among the group there, but it was too late for regrets, so he grabbed the nearest worker and asked him if he'd seen Ryan.

"I think he's with Tess," the guy said, waggling his eyebrows.

"You know where?"

"Try the screening room," the guy said, then returned to his mail.

Seth walked down to the screening room and went inside. It was empty. He turned to go, when he heard a giggle coming from the projectionist's booth.

Seth walked over and cautiously opened the door.

Ryan was sitting in a big, cushy recliner, with Tess on his lap. They were making out, eyes closed, hands roaming.

Embarrassed, Seth took a step back, starting to pull the door closed again, but the floor creaked and Tess opened her eyes and saw him.

"Hey," she said in a friendly voice, disentangling herself from Ryan.

"I'm sorry," Seth said, taking another step back. "I didn't mean to barge in on you."

"It's okay," Ryan said, and Tess nodded.

"We were going to come find you, anyway."

Seth cocked an eyebrow, and Tess laughed. "Don't be pervy. I just wanted to make sure you're coming out with us tomorrow night."

"What's tomorrow night?"

"That band thing at the grocery store you wanted to go to," Ryan reminded him.

"It's not a grocery store, it's Arlene's Grocery, which is a totally cool club downtown," Tess said, then looked at Ryan quizzically. "I thought you told him about it."

"He told *me*," Ryan said. "Anyway, the whole gang is going. You'll have the best time."

"I hope so," Seth said, "because right now I'm having the worst. I'm thinking I should just quit."

"You can't quit," Ryan said. "We only have one more day."

"Exactly. So why am I spending it putting up with this crap?"

"Sandy'll kill you if you quit."

"Besides," Tess said, "if you stick it out, Marco will write you a really good recommendation, and you can come back and intern here again when you're in college."

"And next time, you'll know better than to get yourself roped into being someone's whipping boy," Ryan added.

"I guess I could put up with Milla for a little longer. . . ."

"That's the spirit!" Tess cheered and, leaving

them to get back to their smooching, Seth set off to look for Leah.

He found her sitting behind a desk in the accounting department, obscured by a wall of invoices piled in front of her.

"My god," Seth said, "I thought *my* job sucked."

Leah smiled at him. "At least here no one screams at me when I want to take a break."

"Yeah, I'm really sorry about that —" he started, but Leah shook her head.

"Don't be. The way the bands treat interns is legendary. It's not just you. Or her, for that matter. It's like everyone who comes to guest VJ has a contest to see who has the worst temper."

"Well, I think I know who came in first."

Leah laughed, and Seth saw his opening. "Listen, what are you doing tomorrow night?"

"I don't have plans," she said.

"Well, now you do. There's a concert downtown tomorrow night —"

"Cool —"

"Everyone's going," Seth said, and Leah's face fell.

"Everyone? Like the other interns?"

"Yeah," Seth said, remembering too late how they treated her.

"I don't want to go anywhere with those guys," Leah said in a quiet voice, and Seth touched her arm.

"You won't. You'll be going with me."

18

If Marissa stayed absolutely quiet during breakfast, perhaps neither of the adults would realize that she was hungover. It was a full house. Morgan and Kyle had come over early for an all-day hike and picnic at Haleakala. And Morgan wanted to make sure they all had a hearty meal to start the day. Eggs, sausage, potatoes, muffins.

As each platter passed by Marissa, she felt a wave of nausea.

"Try the eggs, honey. Morgan makes them with chives and feta," Jimmy urged.

"Uh, I had a ton of popcorn last night at the movie. I'm really not that hungry yet." As long as Marissa had a good reason and wasn't snubbing Morgan's food, Jimmy was willing to let it go.

"Don't worry. We'll be taking plenty of food with us. Marissa can have a nice big lunch later," Morgan assured them.

Why was it that everything that came out of Morgan's mouth was so annoying? Marissa wondered. She didn't need this woman fussing over her. Especially since it was only to impress Jimmy with how nurturing she was, or some such nonsense.

Marissa just wanted to go back upstairs, take off her clothes, and crawl back into bed. Clothes. *Her bra.* Oh, damn — she had completely forgotten.

"Something wrong?" Jimmy inquired.

Marissa tried to collect her thoughts. "I . . . I think I left something behind at the movie theater yesterday . . . a pen. I left behind my good . . . pen."

Summer gave Marissa a meaningful look. "I found your 'pen' on our way out. I stuck it in your underwear drawer."

Kyle bolted from the table with a quick "excuse me."

But Marissa could see that he was about to bust out laughing. *Damn him.*

Jimmy and Morgan didn't notice anything going on. They were wrapped up, discussing the previous night's dinner. "Those had to be the best egg rolls I have ever tasted," Morgan raved. "I've been thinking about taking a Chinese cooking class. I've already taken French and Mexican classes. It's always nice to add new dishes to surprise you boys with."

Jimmy stroked her arm. "You could open an international restaurant with everything you know how to cook. Is there nothing you can't do?"

Morgan and Jimmy gazed into each other's eyes with such puppy-dog affection that Marissa knew that spending the rest of the day with them was out of the question.

"I think I'm going to stay at home today. I'm getting a headache," Marissa announced.

Summer and Morgan both shifted in their seats uneasily. Kyle had returned to the room and was hovering in the doorway. Jimmy's face hardened.

"That's it, Marissa. Now, I've had about enough. I can't understand why you're acting like this when we have so few days together, and you're going to spend them all sulking and hiding. The end of your trip will be here before you know it, and we won't have had any kind of real visit."

Jimmy had slammed his own daughter in front of these outsiders! Marissa's fury and heartache came pouring out. "The sooner I leave, the better for you! I hadn't realized what an inconvenience I was going to be to your full, busy life or I never would have bothered coming."

Jimmy still had no idea what Marissa was raving about. "Inconvenience? I've been looking forward to this visit for months. I took the week off work so that we could spend time together."

Marissa folded her arms in disbelief. "Then why haven't we spent any time together?"

"We spend time together every day," he replied.

"No. You spend time together with your new 'family.' And if I'm lucky, I get to hang out in the same room while you have a good time with them. But it's no big deal to take me out of the equation. You won't even notice I'm gone." Marissa was near tears.

Morgan wished she knew how to help. "I'm so sorry that there's been any kind of misunderstanding, Marissa. Your father and I just wanted you to feel at home here."

Marissa turned to Morgan fiercely. "You can't welcome me to this home. It isn't your home."

This brought a swift response from Jimmy. "I will not allow you to speak like that to Morgan. She has been nothing but kind to you, and she is a very important part of my life."

Marissa corrected him. "Not just very important. She's the most important part of your life. Her and Kyle. They're what you care about now. And everyone else — including me — are just people you used to know way back when."

Marissa jumped up from the table and ran straight out the front door.

The others looked at one another in stunned silence. Kyle was the first to collect his wits. "I'll go get her. She can't have gone far. . . . And you know what, why don't you three go to Haleakala? Really. Try to have a good time. I'm going to talk to her."

Jimmy shook his head. "I need to talk to her, too."

"Not right now," Kyle insisted gently. "She feels outnumbered. One-on-one is the best way to start."

Summer stood up. "If I witness any more explosions today, I swear to God, they better be coming from a volcano. I vote for Haleakala."

Morgan touched Jimmy's arm reassuringly. She had great faith in Kyle. Jimmy nodded reluctantly.

Marissa hadn't even taken her purse. And she didn't have a car. In her state of mind, she would want to be in familiar surroundings. Even if only newly familiar. Kyle guessed that he would probably find her in the same park where they first met. And there she was. Same bench.

Kyle sat down gingerly at the other edge of the bench, almost like he was approaching a skittish wild animal. "They're going to head out to the park," Kyle began.

Marissa knew that she had been right. *Of course. They're all relieved that I won't be there.*

Kyle slid a little closer. "Me — I decided not to go. I would much rather go for a horseback ride today. Care to join me?" he asked.

"I don't need any company," Marissa declared.

"But I do," Kyle replied. "I would love some company, Marissa."

Marissa had run out of excuses and out of energy.

Kyle seized the opportunity. "You look really tired. Why don't you go back home? Get some sleep. Have a little bite to eat before we go riding. I'll come get you at three o'clock. Sound okay?"

Marissa didn't say anything. Kyle decided to take that as a yes.

"So, I'm headed back to my place now. But I'll be back this afternoon." Kyle backed away as cautiously as he had approached.

What on earth does he want from me? Marissa knew there had to be some kind of ulterior motive. But she really was too tired to figure it out. Another half hour to make sure that everyone had left. Then she'd head back.

Later that day, after a long three-hour nap, Marissa decided, against her better judgment, to go along with Kyle. For two reasons: First was the horse. She remembered from long ago that when it was too hard to deal with the people in her life, her favorite horse could always make her feel better. Second, from that moment until she stepped on the plane for home, Marissa just needed to make the time disappear as quickly as possible. If Kyle became too insufferable, she would call a cab and make her own way back.

The land surrounding the stables was miles of cool green pasture. Kyle tried to talk Marissa into an older laid-back horse, but she was immediately drawn to Cocoa, a deep brown Arabian with plenty of high spirits. She looked very much like Marissa's old companion, Andiamo.

Marissa immediately pushed Cocoa into a hard gallop. It felt good and there was also the hope that she might be able to leave Kyle behind.

No such luck.

Kyle was never more than a few feet away, and after a while, Marissa had to slow down to give her horse a rest.

They rode silently side by side for a minute

before Kyle spoke up. "Will you hear me out?" Kyle asked.

What could she do? Things couldn't get any worse than they had gotten that morning. Besides, as much as she hated to admit it, the ride had softened her mood. "Don't bore me and don't tick me off," Marissa warned.

"Okay," Kyle began. "I told you that my parents got divorced when I was eleven. Well, Mom didn't want to make things any harder on me than they already were. So, she didn't even let me know when she started dating. She knew it would upset me. It's irrational, but that's the way young kids are."

"Did you just call me an irrational young kid?" Marissa interrupted.

Kyle laughed and shook his head. "Do *not* attempt to read between the lines. There are no lines. Okay? Work with me."

Marissa decided to humor him, as long as he didn't try to make it seem as if she was imagining things or making a big deal out of nothing.

"I was fifteen before I met any of the guys she went out with," Kyle continued. "And then I met quite a few of them. They weren't absolute bozos, but I never liked them. One just seemed to take Mom for granted, and another didn't seem to care about her feelings. One of them was a workaholic and always left her waiting by the phone. But there was this one guy I disliked the most — he struck me as such a pretentious jerk. I had no idea what my mother saw in him.

"But I couldn't help but notice, all of a sudden, that she was smiling all the time. Day and night. Like I hadn't seen her smile in years. So, what could I do? I had to deal with him. I had to spend time with him."

Marissa could see a major lecture coming on. "Well, aren't you the martyr? But I really don't see why anyone should have to subject themselves to the company of someone who's driving them crazy."

Kyle was sorely tempted to find out exactly what he and his mother had done to drive Marissa crazy. But he thought better of it.

"He wanted to play hoops. So we played hoops. He wanted to go fishing. Not really my idea of a swinging time, but we went fishing. We talked. And surprise, surprise. He was actually a pretty cool dude. He was even game when I asked if he'd like to learn how to ride a horse. And this pretentious jerk actually turned out to be one of the best people who could possibly have walked into my mother's and my life."

Kyle stopped to see how Marissa was taking all this. Was she hearing what he was really saying?

"I'll thank you not to keep referring to my father as a pretentious jerk," she said wryly.

But Kyle could see that she wasn't mad at him.

"And we do get along great. That's a bonus for me. But even if we had never hit it off, I would always have been grateful to him for making my mother so happy. Every time I see her smile and remember how difficult those first few years were for her. How hard it was to find someone who didn't hurt her and who really makes her feel loved. I feel completely grateful to Jimmy. I really do."

Marissa pulled her horse to a stop and slid off. She leaned into Cocoa, weighed down by a flood of regret. *Of course Dad deserves to be happy. Why wasn't it enough for me to see him happy?*

"My mom and I — we're not trying to take your dad away from you. We couldn't even if we wanted to. You know, not a single day has passed since I met Jimmy that he hasn't talked about you."

Marissa hadn't known that. "Really?" she said, sniffling.

"He even guessed you'd pick Cocoa as your mount — he said she looked just the same as Andiamo."

"He told you my horse's name?" Marissa asked, surprised. Hell, she was surprised he even remembered the animal's name to begin with.

Kyle laughed again. "Are you kidding? He's told me *everything.* When you were little you had a blue sundress with frogs on it that you'd never take off. You love math but are terrible at history. You didn't want to be a debutante but you did it for your mom —"

"I can't believe he's told you so much about me."

"Why wouldn't he? You're it for him. You're what he cares about." Kyle hesitated, then spoke his next words in a careful, quiet voice. "But when you're not here, you don't want him to be lonely and miserable, do you?"

"Of course not," Marissa said, starting to sob. "I love him. He's my dad."

Kyle rubbed Marissa's shoulder, waiting for her tears to subside. "Then let him be happy."

Marissa wiped her eyes on the handkerchief Kyle handed her. "They're probably home now. Shall we head back?"

Marissa nodded wordlessly, climbing back on her horse. Sure they could go back to the house. But could things possibly be made right? After everything Marissa had put them through, maybe it was just too late.

19

Seth's last day at work was surprisingly uneventful. Milla mostly ignored him, which was a relief, and when it was time to leave, she was nowhere to be found. So Seth asked one of her bandmates to say good-bye for him, surprising himself by feeling a twinge of disappointment that he didn't get to tell her himself.

The boys had dinner at the hotel with Sandy, who had tickets for a Broadway show that evening. Sandy gave them extra cash for cabs and, admonishing them to be careful and have fun, sent them on their way.

Arlene's Grocery was on Stanton Street in the Lower East Side, on a block lined with bars and tiny fashionable shops. They were meeting Leah around the corner at the Pink Pony, a coffee shop that had been around since the sixties.

"You look amazing," Seth said when he saw Leah, and it was true. Her funky fashions and casual braids that looked so out of place in the casual atmosphere of MTV were perfect for this neighborhood, where everyone was grooving in artsy black skirts and retro shirts and fun, clunky shoes.

"Thanks," Leah said. She smiled at Ryan and they set off down the street.

"Arlene's started out as a grocery store," she told them, eliciting a "ha!" from Ryan, who shot an I-told-you-so look at Seth. "But then it closed down and became a crack house before they eventually turned it into a club."

"It was a crack house?" Seth asked dubiously, but Leah squeezed his hand.

"You'll love it. I promise."

They got to the club and went in the door. Inside it was smaller than Seth would have imagined, although come to think of it, he had zero idea how big crack houses usually were. There was a long wooden bar running along one side of the packed room, and a small stage at the front, where a band was already wailing away. People were dancing in the contained shuffle that a crush of bodies necessitates, and the lights were dim, casting a pinkish glow over everyone inside.

Ryan looked around — Tess was standing with a group of interns, drinking beer and swaying to the music. When she spotted the other three kids, her face broke into a huge grin and she waved them over.

Ryan strode through the crowd of people and gave her a warm kiss, but Leah hung back. "Let's just hang out by ourselves," she whispered to Seth.

"Okay, if that's what you want to do," he said.

"But this is a chance for you to get to know the other interns. Ryan says a lot of them are actually really nice, and you do have to work with them for a couple more months."

Leah glanced at the group again, then shook her head. "No, I don't want to —" she started, but was interrupted by Tess, who marched over and grabbed Leah's hand, pulling her toward the group.

Leah looked helplessly at Seth, who followed the pair over to where the other kids were standing.

"That's such a cool shirt," Tess said to Leah. "Don't you guys think so?" She glanced around at the other interns, almost daring them to say something mean.

"Um, yeah, Leah. It's great," said Emily.

Tess gave Diane a sharp nudge with her elbow, and Diane forced a smile. "Yeah, your shoes are cute, too. Where'd you get them?"

"I found this great sample store in Tribeca," Leah told her. "They have all the top designers for, like, eighty percent off."

"Do they have Manolos?" Diane asked, her smile definitely less forced.

"They've got everything — I bought a pair of Manolos there last week — sixty bucks."

"No way!" Diane gasped. "Will you take me? Maybe on Monday at lunchtime?"

"Me too!" Emily piped up.

"Sure," Leah said, the tension leaving her thin shoulders. "I'd be happy to."

"Cervezas!" Marco said, coming over to them. He passed beers around to all the kids, then clinked his bottle against Leah's. She smiled, clinked back, and the stage was set for a perfect evening.

The kids spent an hour dancing to the music, then the band stopped playing and the lights came up onstage. A guy in a grungy plaid shirt walked to the center of the stage and leaned into the microphone.

"Ladies and gentlemen, I'm thrilled to announce we have a surprise guest tonight. Can you put your hands together to welcome, all the way from Glasgow, Milla MacNeil and the Cutters!"

Seth looked at Ryan, his mouth dropping open in surprise. There was no getting away from the woman! Onstage, Milla came bounding out, smiling as she took the mic from the announcer and launched into a song from the Cutters' new CD.

The crowd cheered and started to dance, the interns all pushing to the front of the dance floor. Now it was Seth's turn to hang back — the last thing in the world he needed was for Milla to start screaming at him here, in front of all his new friends.

But Leah was moving along with the group, and Seth's desire to stay close to her outweighed his fear of Milla spotting him. He sidled up to Leah and put his hands on her waist, the two of them moving together to the music. Seth was as happy as he could remember being in a long time, until the Cutters finished their song. When Milla spoke into

135

the mic again, Seth glanced up at the stage, and knew in an instant that he'd been spotted.

"I'm in town this week to be on MTV, and I see a gang here from the station," she said, and the interns went wild, cheering and high-fiving one another. But Milla wasn't done yet. "And who do I spy trying to hide behind that pillar but my assistant. He's afraid if I see him I'll make him work." The crowd laughed, and Seth felt the heat rising on his face. "But there's no work tonight," Milla shouted, "only music. So, Seth, why don't you come up here and help me with this next song?"

Nothing could have surprised Seth more. But the crowd was parting to make room for him to go up to the stage, and friendly hands were pushing him forward.

In a daze, Seth walked up onstage and, under the noise of the crowd applauding, Milla leaned close to him. "I think you'll appreciate this next song," she whispered in his ear.

The band launched into a cover of the Violent Femmes' "Kiss Off," and Milla gave Seth a wicked smile as she started in on the lyrics.

Seth looked out into the crowd. Everyone was dancing again, having a fantastic time. He caught Ryan's eye, who gave him a big thumbs-up, then Leah, who blew a kiss at him.

Milla moved aside to make room for Seth at the mic, and he sang the "yeah, yeah"s at the end of each line of the chorus, getting another gigantic cheer from the MTV gang.

The song ended, and Milla gave Seth a big hug. "You can be my assistant anytime you want," she told him, and Seth smiled.

"No thank you," he answered, shouting over the din, but the smile they exchanged was friendly and conspiratorial, and Seth left the stage, not regretting a single second of his time at MTV.

20

Marissa thought that the others hadn't gotten back yet. Jimmy's car was nowhere to be seen. But he had simply dropped Summer off first and then taken Morgan home. He needed a chance to talk to Morgan alone and do his best to explain Marissa's outburst. Which was pretty difficult, since he couldn't even really explain it to himself.

Marissa was relieved to find Summer alone. She still had no idea what she could possibly say to her father to make things right.

She found Summer lounging in the living room, drinking iced tea and flipping through some colorful tourist catalogs.

Summer looked up to see Marissa at the doorway. "Coop. You missed out big-time. I mean, waterfalls and volcanoes. That's not really something you can see back home. Except at Disneyland. But this was eight thousand times better."

Marissa sat down next to Summer and dropped her head on Summer's shoulder. "I know I missed out. I ruined everything. I promised you'd have a great time, and now it's almost time for us to leave, and I managed to spoil your whole break."

Summer was too happy to see her friend moving back toward normal to give her a hard time. "Oh, you know, between the sailing and the surfing and the gorgeous sunsets and the luau and the smokin' tour guide at the volcano . . . I can honestly say that this week didn't totally suck."

Marissa was very surprised but grateful to hear that Summer didn't consider the week to have been a disaster.

"I could have done without the frat party, though," Summer added. "You owe me big for that. You ready to pay up?"

Marissa nodded eagerly. "Tomorrow. Eleven o'clock. Hula lessons." Summer said.

There was no way that Marissa would have agreed to cheesy hula lessons, except under these circumstances.

"All right. But could we keep this under wraps? The folks back home don't need to hear about this," Marissa replied after only a moment's hesitation.

Summer got up and started swaying in her own hula interpretation. "Oh, Zach is going to hear about this, all right. He's going to get a front-row demonstration."

Knowing that Summer had been holding off on getting intimate with Zach, Marissa wasn't sure this was such a good idea. "A private hula dance might get Zach a little too excited. I know that's not what you want right now."

Summer flopped down in a nearby armchair and faced Marissa. "Actually, I've changed my mind. Zach and I need to take things to the next level."

Marissa wasn't shocked, but she was more than a little confused. "I don't understand. When did you decide this? That is, I guess I know when. Sometime during my self-absorbed meltdown. So, I guess the question is, why?"

"Because Zach is a great guy. I've met a dozen guys this weekend and none of them was better than Zach. It's just stupid to assume that there's someone better waiting in the wings. Because you know what's out there? Dull guys. And eye candy minus the brains. And college boys who hang out at keggers waiting for drunk girls to take off their bras."

Marissa cringed. "I did not take off my bra. It was removed during this game in the pool. . . ." Marissa clarified.

Summer brushed off the explanation. "Yeah, yeah, yeah. Wardrobe malfunction. Whatever. But, getting back to *me* . . ." she said emphatically.

Marissa's mind wandered again for just a moment. What a terrible friend she had been. She wasn't the only person with problems and issues. Summer had been wrestling with a major decision and Marissa hadn't been there for her. She did her best to listen now.

"The thing is, Coop, sex is kind of a big deal. And the fact that I've only done it with Cohen is a huge problem. That's why I can't get his stupid grin and his stupid eyes and his stupid voice out of my mind. But if Zach and I get together, then he and I will be a hundred percent, and this whole Cohen thing will just fade away. Good plan?"

Marissa wasn't so sure. But who was she to offer advice? She just owed it to Summer to support whatever she thought was best for her own life. And if she made a mistake, they would get through it. Together.

Marissa heard Jimmy pounding before she even entered the kitchen. He was tenderizing steaks with a mallet.

He spotted Marissa out of the corner of his eye. "Thought we'd fire up the grill tonight," he said casually.

Marissa stood awkwardly across from him at the kitchen island as Jimmy continued to pummel the steaks.

"Boy, you must be really mad at those steaks," Marissa joked feebly. "They must have been very, very bad cows."

Jimmy looked up cautiously. There was something different in Marissa's voice. Something he hadn't heard for days. "I'm not mad. Just . . . sad, I guess. Sad, and confused, and feeling a little idiotic, I suppose."

Knowing that she had been the cause of all her father's pain was unbearable. Marissa couldn't hold back the tears.

"No, no, no." Jimmy hadn't wanted to make things worse. He quickly washed his hands in the sink and pulled Marissa to the kitchen table. "I was only trying to say that there was some better way of responding to things and I just couldn't find it. I wish I were a wiser man and a better father. And I wish I knew the right thing to do. I should have seen this coming. I was lost in my own little world."

It wasn't enough to undo all the trouble she had caused, but Marissa was at least determined to take full responsibility for this. "It wasn't you. You didn't do anything except to take all the terrible things that happened last year and decide to move on instead of being destroyed by it. It was me who was being selfish and insane. For reasons that don't even make sense to me."

"Honey —" Jimmy tried to interrupt.

"No, Dad. I need to say this . . . I was thinking the other day about getting away from it all. Being on my own and going to college. Maybe it'll be everything it's supposed to be. New people. Great friends. A fantastic guy."

Marissa and Jimmy shared a little smile.

"Are there any classes at this college of yours?"

"Okay. Classes. Sure. But let's say that I felt at home and was having a great time. And you came for a visit and saw that I was happy and excited about my new life. You would be thrilled for me. You know you would. You wouldn't think, 'How dare she be happy without me?'"

Jimmy put his arm around her. "I might feel a twinge," he admitted.

"No. You would have done exactly what fathers are supposed to do," Marissa persisted. "And I should have done the same."

Jimmy, however, didn't feel as if he deserved to get off scot-free. Marissa had been going through some world-class growing pains, and it had completely escaped his notice. How to account for his own tunnel vision?

"Marissa, I made a mess of my life. As you know. Fraud. Almost winding up in jail. I let everyone down. Family, friends, clients who trusted me. When I came to Hawaii, I was really running away from all my mistakes. I had no expectations. And then . . . I find out that life really can start over again. That I don't deserve to be punished forever. To be happy again. Not because the new people are better than the old people. But because my life has more integrity now. I really do want to share this part of my life with you. I want you to be proud of me again."

"I've never stopped being proud of you," Marissa said, her voice cracking. Jimmy pulled her into a warm hug, both of them overcome with emotion. After a minute, Marissa pulled back and looked her father in the eye.

"So, would it be safe to say that you're a man who believes in second chances?" she asked.

"Absolutely," Jimmy responded.

Marissa let out a big sigh. "Glad to hear it."

Jimmy patted Marissa on the arm and got up to finish dinner.

Marissa noticed that he still looked as if something was troubling him. What did she expect? Of course he would need some time before he could really forgive her.

The next day was their last full day in Maui. Marissa had promised herself that she was going to pretend to enjoy the hula class for Summer's benefit. She did owe Summer that much. Friendship was almost as tight a bond as marriage. Richer or poorer. Sickness and health. Summer had stuck through a threat of "poorer" and a heavy-duty mental flip-out — definitely a kind of sickness.

The next day, Marissa was fully expecting to find a giggly class of little girls and middle-aged tourists. But Summer had done her homework. She brought Marissa and Jimmy to one of the largest of Hawaii's annual hula festivals. There were competitions, and performances, and classes throughout the day. Marissa felt a bit foolish not to have known more about the culture she had been visiting for a whole week.

However, Summer had become something of an expert. "This Queen Ka'ahumanu made hula dancing illegal and it was forbidden for the next sixty years. That woman *so* did not deserve to have a mall named after her."

Apparently the queen had taken issue with the skimpy costumes and the celebration of native religions. But Summer and Marissa both agreed during one of the men's competitions, "What's wrong with skimpy?"

By the time they got around to their own dancing lesson, Marissa was actually psyched. The drumming and chanting were infectious. And it was fun to find out that every movement meant something. Water, and courage, and protection, and devotion. When she had agreed to a dance lesson, Marissa never dreamed it would include all these stories and sign language and island history. Jimmy watched from nearby, amused. Marissa was glad that they were spending their last day here. If only this were the beginning of her visit instead of the end.

They got back to the house late that afternoon. "So, what should we do for dinner?" Marissa asked.

"That's up to you two," Summer responded. "I've got plans for the night."

Marissa was puzzled. "Plans? You have dinner plans?" "Yeah, honey," Jimmy explained. "Summer's going to get something with Kyle so that you and I have a chance to spend your last night here together. Just you and me, kiddo. How does that sound?"

It was exactly what she had wanted to hear all

week. "It sounds great, Dad," Marissa said. And it was definitely the perfect way to end her vacation. Or was it?

Marissa couldn't stop remembering the lingering worries on her father's face last night.

Marissa stepped out onto the front porch for privacy. Maybe this was going to be pointless, but she had to give it a try. She used Jimmy's cell phone. It wasn't difficult to find his most frequently dialed number.

"Kyle. Hi. It's Marissa." She could hear the smile in Kyle's voice.

"I don't think I know a Marissa. At least not one who would be calling me."

"Very funny. Why I really called is to talk to your mother. But just a sec. I also . . . never thanked you for getting me out of that party. It was a really stupid situation to get into."

"Don't mention it," Kyle responded.

"And I also wanted to thank you for yesterday. For the riding and . . . everything."

"I'm going to infect you with a little aloha spirit, Marissa, if it's the last thing I do," Kyle declared. "Hey, here's my mom."

Marissa took a deep breath. She really had no right to expect anything from this woman. "Morgan. Hi. I'm just calling to see if you and Kyle would join me and Dad and Summer for dinner."

A moment of silence that filled Marissa with

dread. "I know it's your last night together, and I would never want to intrude on that," Morgan finally said.

"It's not an intrusion. It would be a huge favor to me, really. Because otherwise, I'll go home knowing I've been the world's most ridiculously obnoxious and ungracious brat, and it will haunt me for the rest of my days. I know you're too kind to leave me to that fate."

"You're being way too hard on yourself. But I suppose . . . I suppose if you really don't mind us being there . . ." Morgan began.

Marissa interrupted. "And by the way, Dad didn't ask me to call. I'd really like you to be there."

Funny how you could tell when people were smiling at the other end of the line.

Marissa joined Jimmy at the back of the house. He was planting seeds in about half a dozen ceramic pots. "What's that?" Marissa inquired.

"Oh, just some herbs. Sage. And basil. Morgan . . ." Jimmy's voice trailed off. "Morgan likes to have fresh stuff to cook with when she's over here."

Marissa smiled. "Say, Dad. Did Morgan ever hear that I said she was a —"

"A Betty Crocker-slash-geisha mutant. No, I don't believe I ever mentioned that," Jimmy replied. "You did seem a little out of sorts that first night and she wondered if she had done anything wrong."

"What did you say?" Marissa asked.

"I said it was probably cramps."

"You didn't!" Marissa punched her father in the arm. "I'm surprised she didn't whip me up some homemade medicinal," she teased.

Jimmy pulled his jacket over, reached into a pocket, and flipped a baggie of dried herbs onto Marissa's lap. "Steep for ten minutes and take four times a day until discomfort subsides," he recited.

Marissa's mouth dropped open. "How does this not scare you?"

Jimmy grinned good-naturedly. He knew that Morgan did take a little getting used to.

"Anyhow, it's time for you to get cleaned up," Marissa told her father. "Morgan and Kyle will be joining us for dinner."

The look on Jimmy's face was truly priceless.

"Get a move on," Marissa urged. "I said we'd pick them up by six."

Fortunately, Summer, Kyle, and Morgan didn't mind another luau. No such thing as too many luaus.

Marissa felt lucky that she wasn't going to miss this quintessential Hawaiian feast after all. In the little bit of time she had left there, she didn't want to miss anything.

It was like being at a birthday party, with colorful leis instead of party hats. "You know, as long as I've been living here, I have never actually been over to see that hula festival. Did you all have a good time?" Morgan inquired.

"It was really beautiful," Marissa said.

"What she means is, the men were really beautiful," Summer joked.

"They were," Marissa admitted, "but I meant the whole thing. The stories. The ceremony. There's really nothing like it back home."

"It's a special place," Morgan agreed.

"Try the poi, Coop. It's disgusting, but it's just one of those things you have to try," Summer insisted.

"Marissa couldn't even eat oatmeal when she was a baby," Jimmy informed them. "I can't see that poi is going to stand a chance."

"It had a weird texture," Marissa protested.

"The odd thing is, she was fine with Cream of Wheat. So, actually, this might be right up her alley," Jimmy added.

Kyle nodded approvingly. "Bring on the poi," he agreed.

The pleasant evening was such a contrast to the turbulence of the past week. At first Marissa had been afraid that Morgan was just pretending to like her for Jimmy's sake. Who could blame her for holding a grudge? But it really didn't seem as if she was acting. Any woman who pretends not to date for four years so that she doesn't freak her adolescent son out — Marissa had to consider the possibility that Morgan was simply a genuinely nauseatingly caring person. As for Jimmy, Marissa had never seen him happier.

"Marissa, what was that ride we got so dizzy on, we had to sit down for half an hour afterward?" Jimmy asked.

"Dad, I thought we made a pact never to

discuss this. . . . All right. All right. It was the Teacups," Marissa admitted, sharing in his memories.

"I'd love to give you a hard time, but those Teacups are no joke," Kyle said.

They laughed. And they ate. And Marissa marveled and regarded them all with humble amazement — whether or not she deserved it, she had been forgiven.

21

On their way to the airport the next morning, Sandy told the limo driver to make a stop along the way.

"We never made it to the top of the Empire State Building," Sandy told the boys as the car cruised to a stop in front of the giant monolith.

They went in the front doors into the giant stone lobby. There was a bulletin board that read ESTIMATED WAIT TIME: 4 HOURS in press-on letters. Ryan pointed it out.

"Four hours? We'll miss our plane," Seth said, dismayed, but Sandy smiled and pulled three passes out of his pocket.

"I've already taken care of it," he said, and led them to an elevator that whisked them to the top with no wait at all.

Ryan, Sandy, and Seth stepped out onto the broad walkway around the top of the tower. Manhattan lay below them, a 360-degree expanse of buildings and trees and life.

"Wow," Ryan breathed. "This is — spectacular."

"Think of everything that's going on out there,"

Seth said, joining him at the rail. "All the poss-
ibilities."

"Like for love?" teased Ryan. He had seen Seth
and Leah kissing in a darkened corner of the club
last night.

Both the boys had spent as long as possible
with the girls they met, staying in the club until it
closed, then walking back across town to the hotel
instead of taking a cab.

As bittersweet as it was to leave, Leah and Tess
had both given them their phone numbers, and all
four were determined to get together again,
maybe in the summer, maybe when they went to
college. In any event, all four of them were happy
to hold the memory of their weeklong romance
close.

"Maybe." Seth shrugged, answering Ryan's
question. "But also — college and music and staying out all night, going to clubs and meeting
people and hailing cabs."

"Running errands, walking the dog," Ryan
added, and Seth grinned.

"Getting caught fooling around at work."

"Singing backup with a band."

"Getting tattoos and Mohawks —"

"Buying comic books —"

"— Jousting!"

They both laughed and were still smiling when
Sandy came over to them. He put his arms around
their shoulders and leaned against the rail, looking
over the city to Central Park.

"Thanks, Sandy," Ryan said suddenly. "This trip was amazing."

"Completely." Seth nodded. "I couldn't have asked for more."

"Well, maybe we'll all come back here one day," Sandy said. "But in the meantime, that view'll have to hold you."

The three guys took one last look, then headed toward the elevators.

"All set?" Sandy asked, and Ryan hesitated.

"Do we have time to drive past the Statue of Liberty on our way to the airport?"

"We'll make time," Sandy said, and the elevator doors opened and they stepped inside.

22

Morgan and Kyle came to the airport to see the girls off. While Jimmy said his good-bye to Summer, Marissa and Kyle had their final exchange. He gave her a quick hug. "See ya later, sis. . . . Just kidding," he added.

"Aloha, Kyle," Marissa deadpanned, pushing him away. *Hmmm. Big brother Kyle. Kind of preposterous. But oddly enough, not freakin' me out.*

Morgan was next. She looked pretty anxious, Marissa thought. Not quite sure where she stood.

"I'm so sorry you weren't able to make it to Haleakala. It's one of my favorite places on the whole island."

Standing there, it was hard for Marissa to remember that she had ever blamed this woman for taking anything away from her.

"Next time," Marissa said, meaning it. Morgan hugged her, both of them hugely relieved.

Everyone stood aside to let Marissa and Jimmy have a few final moments of privacy.

"Dad . . . I . . . I . . ." Marissa didn't even know where to begin.

"No need to say anything. As it so happens, your father is an extraordinarily talented mind reader." Jimmy bent down, touched his forehead to Marissa's, and then pulled back. "Apology accepted. Say no more." He touched her forehead again. "You're going to do your best to be happy for me. Glad to hear it. And I think there was one last thought rattling in your brain."

They touched foreheads one more time. Jimmy pulled away with a mischievous smile. "Yes, I actually have dropped a few pounds. Thanks for noticing."

Marissa threw her arms around Jimmy, laughing and crying. How did she get to be so lucky?

23

Five hours later, two planes landed at the John Wayne Airport in Orange County.

Marissa and Summer debarked at the Air Hawaii gate and headed downstairs to the baggage claim to pick up their suitcases.

Ryan, Seth, and Sandy dragged their carry-on bags through the gate at the American Airlines terminal. Sandy left the boys with the luggage and went to fetch the car from the long-term parking lot and pick them up.

The girls retrieved their bags and took the escalator back up to the exit level, where they would look for a cab to take them back to Newport.

If they looked to their left, over the railing and across the concourse, they would have seen Seth and Ryan, sitting on a bench by the doors, waiting for Sandy to pick them up. But Marissa was rummaging through her purse for a pack of gum, and Summer was examining the ends of her hair to see what havoc the salty ocean water had wreaked on her ends.

Neither of them noticed the boys.

If Ryan and Seth had lifted their heads, they could have spotted the girls just as easily. But Ryan was watching out the door for Sandy's car, and Seth was staring at the piece of paper with Leah's phone number, trying to commit it to memory. So they didn't see the girls, either.

Once the best of friends, the four passed within feet of one another, but missed one another entirely. It was how they had been all year. None of them liked it that way, and all of them wished they could go back to the way things had been.

But like it or not, they just weren't connecting. And unless something changed, they would keep missing one another long after spring break had ended.